FOOLISH HEARTS

FOOLISH HEARTS
NEW GAY FICTION

EDITED BY
TIMOTHY J. LAMBERT
AND R. D. COCHRANE

Published in the United States by Cleis Press, Inc., 2246 Sixth Street, Berkeley, California 94710.

Printed in the United States.
Cover design: Scott Idleman/Blink
Cover photograph: Valentin Casarsa/Getty Images
Text design: Frank Wiedemann

First Edition.
10 9 8 7 6 5 4 3 2 1

Trade paper ISBN: 978-1-62778-005-6
E-book ISBN: 978-1-62778-018-6

"Bothered, Bewildered," by Rob Williams, originally appeared in *Versal* #4 (2006, Amsterdam).

In memory of Aaron
and of Rex

Contents

INTRODUCTION

All my life I've revered, embraced and celebrated foolishness. It seems strange that we raise our children with vibrant colors, songs, puppets and animated films, and then worry if they hold on to those treasures and take them with them as they grow and wander into the world. I was raised on a steady diet of violin and voice lessons, theater, and library books. Did I go into the Navy or study biochemical engineering? No. I don't even know what that is.

I've never understood the conventional. Why isn't being a musician considered a "real job" by the masses? Why is it considered more acceptable to be doctors or lawyers? Why shouldn't mamas let their babies grow up to be cowboys? My unconventional career choices always fed my creativity, and I love that. I've never wanted a job where I wouldn't be able to walk in one day with blue hair or vinyl trousers if I felt like it.

I can certainly understand the need for stability. My more successful relationships have been with conventional men. There's nothing sexier than a man in a tailored suit, or a man who knows what he wants and why he wants it. As long as a conventional man has passion and responds to the beat of a foolish heart, he's all right by me.

It's not the serious moments of my life that I care to remember. Only the laughter and lighthearted moments can turn my blues into rainbows. I doubt that on my deathbed I'm going to fondly recall that time I took my SATs, or when I filed my first tax return. I'll more likely go back to when Amadeus was rocking Falco and I was in my high school production of Shakespeare's *A Midsummer Night's Dream,* or teenage parties, school dances and making out with Evan in the Art Department's photo darkroom.

The taunts, jeers, physical and mental punishments of youth happened to me. I don't deny that. But I quickly learned that those moments often create beauty. A beautiful musical composition can be born from utter sorrow. Visual feasts by some of the best painters were created while they were slowly dying. If you don't like your life, you can get on a stage and be someone else for a while.

The irony of photographs being born in a darkroom was never lost on me.

When a king or queen wanted amusement, it was the jester who was brought forth. These days, it seems the fools are all around us. We look to one another for amusement. When kids tease or torment each other—often a fine line between the two—it may be done under the guise of kidding around. "I was just kidding!" says the accused. People having painful accidents always receive the greatest laughs and the highest ratings. Physical and mental ailment has become a new art form. People who throw up on television are the new celebrities.

Puck was correct when he claimed that we mortals are fools.

Unless it's been channeled into a comedic stage play, I've never been one to laugh at somebody's pain and suffering. I'd rather laugh at myself. Recently, I was picking up dog poop from my front yard when an attractive man walked by. I said *hi*, he said *hi* back, and I struggled to come up with something meaningful to say, to keep him engaged, to keep him standing in front of me so I could stare into his beautiful brown eyes. I failed. I said nothing more and he walked on. It was only after he left that I realized I was holding a bag of dog shit the entire time. I could certainly laugh at that.

There have been many wonderfully foolish moments in my life. Waltzing on rooftops, making out on beaches at midnight, sneaking into movie theaters, following scavenger-hunt maps to secret warehouse rave parties, one-night stands that lasted for three days and many more too personal to write about here. There are probably just as many *unfortunately* foolish moments. Good or bad, I wouldn't want to miss out on any of the foolishness life has offered, and I certainly hope there will be more to come.

A foolish life is a life well lived, and a foolish heart is a heart well loved.

Timothy J. Lambert
Houston, Texas

HELLO ALOHA

Tony Calvert

Four days in the Magic Kingdom hadn't been my idea of the perfect vacation, but here I was, just finishing my dinner with Br'er Fox. It's not that I don't like Br'er Fox, or any of the characters roaming the dinner hall. I'm not anti-Disney. But banjo-playing bears, singing snakes, and deer named after strippers aren't my thing.

They are Chad's thing though, and when he and Martin decided to "seal the deal," all Chad could talk about was a Disney wedding. As best man it was my duty to be here. I did my best to keep my focus on my plate and ignore the way Pooh Bear was eyeing my honey-roasted chicken.

Chad McKenzie and Martin Bishop were the perfect Disney couple. Martin was tall, with angular features. He shaved his head to hide a receding hairline, but his head was ideally shaped for it. He could easily step into any Disney movie as a master swordsman who seems slightly villainous but proves to be good of heart. Chad was muscular and had a mane of blond hair that always managed to be perfect thanks to the products he liberally applied. His teeth sparkled, as did his dark blue eyes; he looked like a Disney prince who could set anyone's heart pounding.

As the Disney freak in the relationship, Chad had planned everything. First there was the "character dinner" for the wedding party and family. Next were to be two days of theme park goodness. We even had matching T-shirts so anyone in the McKenzie-Bishop wedding party could be easily identified. Finally, the commitment ceremony would take place poolside at the Polynesian Hotel where we were staying: sarongs required. It was a tough decision: Martin could certainly afford the Disney Dream Enchantment wedding, complete with Cinderella coach and footmen. But Chad didn't go to the gym every day for nothing. The chance to show off his princely abs won out.

It was all a bit much.

I'm not bitter, I swear. I love love as much as the next gay; it's just never worked out for me, and I gave up on Prince Charming a long time ago. Three-hundred-forty-seven days ago, in fact.

It was a bad breakup.

I'd thought Michael Stetson was "the one." My sister Jenny thought he was "the one." Even Chad, who never liked my boyfriends, thought he was "the one." The only person in my life who didn't think Michael Stetson was "the one" was Michael Stetson. With a name that reeked of cowboys and cheap cologne, I should have known it, too. Maybe his deep dark eyes or the way he kissed me made me think we were something special. Maybe it was how easily he slipped into my life, sharing my condo and closet space. It wasn't long before we were doing relationship things like picking out new paint for the master bath and debating how to tile the kitchen floor. We quit going to clubs, instead opting for dinner with other couples, the theater, or weekends at the beach. The wildest thing Michael ever wanted was a threesome on Saturdays: me, him and Orville Redenbacher. Orville and I always let him pick the movie. Everything was perfect.

Until it wasn't.

One Monday I came home and found Michael and his suitcase in the kitchen ready to say good-bye. He said things were getting too "real," and he wasn't ready for that. It was time for him to go. He was going to stay with a cousin or an uncle in Idaho to get his mind clear. He assured me it wasn't me, it was him, and then he was gone.

That night, lying alone in my bed, it felt like it was me. Three-hundred-forty-seven days later, it still felt like it was me.

So here I was at another wedding, destined to hang out at the bar with the other lonely-onlys who hadn't managed to get a date, toasting the happy couple while wallowing in my own misery.

Maybe I'm a *little* bitter.

After dinner I found a distant corner to watch the festivities. I couldn't help but smile. Chad was in an animated conversation with Minnie Mouse and Daisy Duck. Martin appeared to be getting sage advice from The Mad Hatter and one of the Tweedles. I could never tell them apart.

I felt a tap on my shoulder.

Great. It was Goofy.

He made a grand gesture toward the rest of the party, indicating that I should join.

"I'm good right here."

He crossed his arms and tapped his foot in what I assumed was an exaggerated imitation of me.

I found myself explaining. "I'm not much of a Disney guy."

Goofy brought his hands to his cheeks like the *Home Alone* kid.

"It's nothing personal. My sister loves you." I hesitated a moment then felt compelled to add, "Really she's a big fan of Pluto. There was this time that my mom came here without us—"

Goofy seemed to gasp.

I nodded. "I know! Who goes to Disney World and leaves the kids at home? Anyway, my sister asked for a stuffed Pluto and my Mom came home with a stuffed Goofy. She said you were both dogs, and that you were the one who reminded her of Jenny. Because you were both goofy, not because my sister has buckteeth and big ears. No offense. Although until she got braces, her teeth were a little big."

Goofy pulled his ears, so I assumed no offense was taken.

"Be honest with me; don't you get tired of these things?"

Goofy shook his head vehemently.

"Oh, come on. First you have to watch people gorge themselves—do you even get to eat?"

He rubbed his belly; I wasn't sure what that meant. Did Goofy eat before the banquet, or was he fed scraps like the good dog that he was?

"Then you have to goof things up, and I'll bet a lot of kids pull on those ears. Plus if it's a wedding, no matter how cute the couple is, you know that about a third of marriages end in divorce."

He shook his head, disagreeing with me. Apparently Goofy was a believer in happily ever after.

"I'm sure Disney couples don't fare much better. How long do you think it took before Prince Eric got all paunchy, stuffing his face on seafood? He probably even ate that singing crab. You know Ariel finally looked across the table and said, 'I gave up my fins for this?'"

Goofy put his hands over his ears as if to drown me out.

"I think this one will last." I gestured toward Martin and Chad. "I don't think they even have statistics for gay marriages."

I had an overwhelming urge to make Goofy actually speak. Maybe I could shock him. "So Goof, we've been talking for a while. I feel like we're friends."

He nodded, put his arm around my shoulder, and gave it a squeeze.

"Be honest with me, which of the princes are gay? I'm saying Charming. Aladdin, for sure. The Beast is pretty straight when he's the actual Beast, but when he turns into a human—totally gay."

Goofy put his hands on his hips for a moment then shook a finger at me.

"Seriously, I've seen Aladdin at a gay bar in Tampa; he has to be." I leaned closer to him. "I wish Prince Philip was, but I don't think he is. Maleficent and Ursula, though? Drag queens. Don't tell me they aren't."

Goofy nodded his head up and down like he was chuckling, and that made me smile. Still, he hadn't said a word. I was going to play dirty.

"Goofy, I heard some Disney gossip." He leaned closer, and I whispered, "Did you hear that Mickey and Minnie are getting a divorce?"

Goofy pulled away and shook his head no.

It was my turn to lean closer. "The judge thought it was because she was insane, but Mickey said, 'Minnie's not crazy. She's fucking Goofy!'"

Goofy whispered back, "Forget Minnie. I'd be more interested in Mickey."

I'd made Goofy speak!

Wait: What did he say? *Goofy* was gay?

Their appearance over, all the characters were waving good-bye. Goofy quickly whispered, "I'll be in front of the Haunted Mansion tomorrow if you want to talk some more." He left me and loped into line with Minnie, Daisy and the others.

Hotel rooms aggravated Chad. Doors locked, and there was nothing he loved more than throwing open a door and making a dramatic entrance. At the Polynesian, he had to knock and wait for me to take my time answering.

Still, when I did, it was dramatic. Chad brushed by me and stood in front of the TV, making sure he had my full atten-tion. "So there I was, having a lovely conversation with Donald Duck, one of my heroes—"

"Donald Duck is one of your heroes?"

Chad nodded. "He walks around all day with no pants and people accept it. I envy his freedom, and that is not the point. I'm talking to Donald, then to Winnie, and I look over and you're talking to Goofy. You talked to Goofy from the moment you finished dinner until the moment the characters left."

"I'm sorry. I should have introduced him."

"I know who Goofy is, no introduction necessary. I invited seven choice, single men to this wedding for you, and you haven't talked to any of them. They'll probably end up hooking up with one another, but they were invited for *you*."

"Not for the wedding gifts?"

Chad smiled. "I'm sure we'll be receiving something, but *mostly* for you."

"I hate matchmaking," I reminded him.

"Jordan."

I knew then that this was serious. Chad usually called me Jory; when he used my entire first name, I was in for a lecture.

"I know you hate the thought of getting your heart broken

again. I'm not saying you have to invite any of the Seven Sexy Singles for a Saturday night with you and Orville; that's sacred. But you could have a little fun. You remember fun, don't you? A little dancing, a little...well, maybe not so little..."

"I'm not ready for dancing or a little."

Chad sighed heavily. "Michael broke your heart, but it's been a year. I hate quoting Barry Manilow, but you have to get ready to take a chance again."

I sighed back at him. "First, you love quoting Barry Manilow. Second, when I'm ready, I'll let you know. I need to do a little more healing. I loved him, Chad."

Chad sat on my bed. "He loved you."

"Yeah, he loved me so much he left."

"He did love you; just because he left doesn't mean he didn't. Sometimes people can't do things even when they think they want to. Love doesn't always go the way we expect or want. That doesn't mean it isn't love. Love isn't perfect. That doesn't mean it isn't worthwhile."

I bit my tongue. It's hard to take advice about the imperfection of love from a man having his wedding in the Magic Kingdom.

He stood. "Just try to be a little more social. You never know."

I followed him to the door. As he stepped into the hall, I asked, "When you say you were talking to Donald Duck, was he talking back?"

Chad grimaced. "Don't be ridiculous. They aren't allowed to talk."

"Oh," I said, and then added, "Goofy actually spoke to me." I shut the door as fast as I could.

"You bitch!" Chad called.

"Nice talk in the Magic Kingdom," I said through the door.

* * *

At breakfast, Chad pointed out the Seven Sexy Singles. I wondered if they'd take back their Cuisinarts and bread makers if they knew how Chad was dissecting their attributes, the best ways to approach them and the things he'd do with them—if he weren't getting married, of course. Somewhere between the bacon and my second cup of coffee, I promised to be more sociable. He had a point, and I really wanted him to shut up.

I was in front of the Haunted Mansion at 11:00 a.m. The question wasn't whether Goofy would be there; he was. The question was: Why was I? What was I expecting from another one-sided conversation with a guy in a dog suit?

He was kneeling, his arms around two kids posing for a picture. Then he "kissed" each one on the cheek before they ran off to greet Chip and Dale.

When Goofy saw me, he waved and motioned for me to join him. He pulled at my shirt.

"Yeah, I'm hard to miss." The shirt was lavender, and in what could only be described as a Tiki font, it read BEST MAN.

Goofy ran his paw underneath the lettering and flexed his muscles. Apparently *he* thought I was the best man, too.

"I only came by to apologize to you. That joke was off color. Not to mention rude. It's not even funny. Although you and Mickey: that was a revelation."

He shook his head. Apparently a night with Mickey was nothing but a pipe dream.

"I was uncomfortable last night. I broke up with a guy about a year ago, and now Chad and Martin are getting married. I needed someone to talk to. And there you were." I winced. "I'm doing it again, yakking away at someone who doesn't yak back."

Goofy gave me a hug and patted my back. He understood.

"You know, Goof, it's not like I'm even in love with him anymore. It's just that starting over is scary. I know if you don't risk something, you don't have a shot at happily ever after, but what if I'm one of the people who doesn't get one? Maybe I'm one of those guys who always gets sent back to the beginning. Do not pass go; do not collect two hundred dollars."

Did Goofy have a working knowledge of Monopoly?

I finished with, "It sucks," more to myself than to my new companion.

Another group came up, and Goofy did his goofy thing. He posed for pictures and waved good-bye when his fans took off in pursuit of another character.

He turned back to me.

"So, yeah, thanks for putting up with me. I'll let you get back to work."

Goofy would have none of it. He took my hand and skipped to his next destination, dragging me behind him.

I saw other lavender shirts throughout the day, but I didn't seek them out. I was having too good a time watching Goofy. Secretly, I hoped he'd talk to me again. His voice had echoed in my head all night, not bad for only two sentences. It was deep, and I imagined him laughing a low strong laugh—which was very un-Goofy.

For the most part, Goofy lived up to his name, goofing with the crowds. I felt as if a little of his magic began to seep inside me. I knew part of it was the costume, but I sensed something special about the man inside. He knew which little girl needed to have her nose tweaked, which little boy wouldn't shy away from a pretend kiss. His silliness made grown men giggle, and when he flirted with women, they blushed. He had a knack for making people feel good—and it went beyond the dog suit.

"Goofy, you never told me: do you believe in happily ever after?"

"There you are!"

Chad. I didn't have to see him to know he was standing behind me, his hands on his hips, all judgey. I turned around, knowing I'd have to come up with an excuse for not chasing down the Seven Sexy Singles.

Chad brushed right by me, going straight to my friend.

"Goofy, I have a bone to pick with you. I'll bet you like bones, don't you?"

Goofy pulled his ears and nodded his head.

"Has Jordan here been bothering you?"

Goofy shook his head.

"I'd say he has a crush on you, only Jordan doesn't get crushes. He's too jaded—bad breakup—but you probably know that, with all the secrets he's been sharing. Has he been sharing secrets?"

Goofy zipped his lip and pretended to throw away the key.

"I have a secret, too." Chad leaned over and whispered something to Goofy that made him dance.

Goofy then made a wild gesture to me, so I joined the two of them.

"I'm stealing you from your doggie friend here, but first I want a picture." Chad pulled out his camera and called, "Say cheese."

Goofy wrapped both his arms around me and pulled me tight. While Chad clicked away, Goofy whispered, "You should believe in happily ever after, too, but you have to take a chance to get there."

Was Goofy a Fanilow, too?

"Sometimes you have to take a few," he added. "Everyone has a heartache."

Chad pulled at my arm the way Goofy had earlier. This time I was a little more reluctant to go along.

We were at the dinner table. Chad clutched imaginary pearls as he relayed the story to Martin. "And there he was, hanging out with Goofy again!" He turned to me. "Honestly, Jory, I had no idea you were a furry."

Martin took a sip of his wine. "How do you even know what a furry is?"

Chad cleared his throat. "I had a life before I met you."

I blurted, "Goofy is gay."

Martin's mouth dropped open.

Chad gasped. "I was only kidding about the furry thing."

"It's not like that. There's something about him that makes me feel good."

Martin raised an eyebrow. "He's a guy in a funny dog suit. It's his job to make you feel good."

"He makes my heart feel a little lighter. It's beyond just Goofy being goofy. He makes me think happy thoughts."

Martin repeated, "He's a guy in a funny dog suit. It's his job to make you feel good."

"Be glad for me. I'm at Disney World. I'm hanging out with Goofy and having fun. Wasn't that what you wanted? For me to have fun?"

"You're hanging out with Goofy and *only* Goofy. You aren't getting any face time with Tigger, Pluto or Captain Hook. Now there's a guy for you, Captain Hook. Tall, dark and handsome." Martin paused. "Although the passionate embraces could be painful."

"Forget the furrys. What about the Seven Sexy Singles I invited just for you? I think two of them already hooked up." Chad narrowed his eyes. "Did they think I wouldn't find out?"

"Did they know they were here for Jordan's pleasure?" Martin asked.

"It's not as if I could put it on the invitation. But they still should have known," Chad added unreasonably.

Martin shook his head. "Jordan, you don't even know what Goofy looks like. He could be—" He broke off. I couldn't tell if he was concerned with offending me or the Disney powers that be.

Chad blurted it out. "Troll! He could be a troll."

That night as I lay in bed, my mind was full of Goofy. Could I really have a crush on a Disney character?

Chad was right. Goofy could be a troll, but for some reason, it didn't matter. His voice, his short whispered sentences, reached into my gut and swirled everything around. He was more than a dog, and troll or not, he was kind. I imagined he was funny. I was imagining a lot of things about my new friend Goofy.

The next morning, Chad didn't let me stray too far from his sight. Judging by the way Sexy Single One gripped Sexy Single Two's thigh in the teacup ride, Chad was right; two of them had hooked up. He was in the cup with us and pursed his lips and turned crimson when he noticed the thigh gripping. *Really,* his expression conveyed, *how dare they!*

We went from there to the Magic Carpet Ride, the Haunted Mansion and the Country Bear Jamboree. In It's A Small World, Chad held my hand and sang along. Occasionally he would grip me a little tighter and say, "Pay attention to the lyrics, Jory. It's a world of hope..."

I wanted to point out that the next line wasn't so cheery, but it was Disney and tomorrow was his wedding day, so I let it go.

I pretended not to look for Goofy as Chad dragged me around the park. Inevitably, when we were leaving the Pirates

League after Martin insisted that we have our faces painted, I ran into him. I was all greasepaint and headscarves.

Curse Martin and his Captain Hook fetish.

Chad looked at me and smiled. "Jory, look who it is! It's your friend Goofy." Goofy gave me that *Home Alone* move.

Chad smirked. "Sorry Goofy, this is the real Jory. He loves to make himself up. Do you like pirates?"

Goofy nodded and patted his heart.

Chad took Martin's hand and led him away. "We'll be over here while you two catch up."

I tried to forget I had a moustache and matching eyebrows drawn on my face.

"Today's my last day here. Tomorrow's the wedding and— that's it."

Goofy kicked the dirt with his oversized shoe.

"But I'll be back when Barnstormer opens. I can't miss the Great Goofini." I didn't really like roller coasters, but it didn't seem cool to disrespect the Goofy roller coaster to Goofy. "Having your own roller coaster must be a big deal around here."

He clapped his hands in excitement.

"So I guess this is good-bye. Thanks for lending me your ears." I hoped Goofy wouldn't make a "Friends, Romans" joke, and he didn't. "It was nice to talk. I don't know why, but I felt a connection with you. Spending yesterday with you was good for me. I guess being Goofy, you get that a lot."

Goofy opened his arms wide and gave me a hug, gripping me close. "I felt a connection, too."

Right then a horde of redheaded children circled us, all of them screaming in Disney delight and tugging at Goofy's pants.

I took a step away and let him get to work. It didn't seem fair to deny children Goofage their parents had bought and paid for.

I joined Chad and Martin and did my best not to appear ruffled.

"Let's get out of here," I said, pulling Chad off the bench.

Martin sniffed. "That was a quick good-bye." The gold earring he'd gotten at Pirate League looked perfect on him.

"There wasn't much to say."

Chad pouted, looking back at Goofy, who was still surrounded by freckled little carrot tops. "But you were crushing on him."

I sighed. "He's just a guy in a dog suit."

The wedding went off without a hitch. Martin and Chad, clad in their best sarongs and shirtless, exchanged vows, did the ring thing and kissed at the end of the ceremony. I'll admit I got a little teary. Chad and Martin had found their happily ever after, and it was beautiful to watch.

Everyone was poolside. The newlyweds were taking on two of the Seven Sexy Singles in a game of chicken. I suspected that kind of roughhousing wasn't allowed on the property, but there was no stopping the two grooms. I sat at a table working on the toast I'd be giving at the luau later that evening. It might be a casual wedding, but Chad still expected certain things from his best man.

"Hey."

I'd just gotten up, intending to practice my toast in the dining room where we'd be later. Chad would want perfection; any mistake I made could go down in history as the toast that ruined his wedding.

The "hey" came from one of the wedding guests who'd stopped at my table.

"Hi," I answered.

He wasn't one of the Singles, but he was cute enough in his board shorts and T-shirt. He was holding one of the gift bags given to the wedding guests. He held out his other hand and said, "My name's Sam."

I shook his hand. "Jordan."

"Working on the toast?" He glanced toward Chad, who was on Martin's shoulders, his arms raised in victory. The Singles never stood a chance. "You have a lot of material to work with."

"Yeah."

"Looks like they're off to a great start."

Chad and Martin were challenging yet another couple. Chicken was turning out to be their game.

"I brought something for you." He handed me the bag. "It was the only gift wrap I could find."

I reached into the bag and pulled out my favorite Disney dog. Realization dawned.

He smiled. "Yeah. Call me Sam."

I looked from him to the stuffed Goofy and back again. I wasn't quite sure what to say.

"Chad invited me. Mickey covered my shift."

I laughed a little. "Mickey?"

"He's a good Mouse that way."

Chad let out a war whoop, there was a splash and the grooms were once again victorious.

Sam looked at them again, then at me and held out his hand. "I think we can take them."

I nodded. "I think we can, too."

I put Goofy back in his bag and took Sam's outstretched hand. It was time to take my chance.

I leaned in and kissed him. He gripped my hand tighter, and my heart began to beat faster.

In the Magic Kingdom, a kiss can awaken a sleeping princess. A kiss can turn a frog into a prince. A kiss can give a voice back to a mermaid.

And sometimes, a kiss can make a man realize that even better than a possible happily ever after is a goofy beginning.

HOW TO BE SINGLE AT A WEDDING

David Puterbaugh

I t was Natalie who said they should write a blog. She told Peter the idea had come to her on the way over from Boston yesterday afternoon, and the blog's title—How to Be Single at a Wedding—arrived as her ferry docked in Provincetown. Peter had no interest in writing a blog. But he liked Natalie and hated to disappoint her. The Hollywood-themed wedding shower he'd cohosted with her the month before—complete with red carpet arrivals, "paparazzi" photos of the guests, and a two-foot-long golden cake in the shape of an Oscar for Best Couple—was proof of that.

The innkeepers at the wedding venue had been very accommodating. After breakfast they'd moved the table and deck chairs from the front porch to the backyard so that decorating could begin under Natalie's supervision. Yards of white chiffon fabric were draped over the wooden railing that enclosed the porch, where it cascaded down the handrails and pooled at the bottom of the brick steps. White paper bells hung in bunches from the porch roof. Roses in an assortment of autumnal colors—barn red, pumpkin orange, golden yellow—had been delivered at 10:00 a.m. by a florist on Bradford Street. Petals were sprinkled along the garden path to the inn's front gate. All the guests staying at the inn that weekend were there for the wedding, and just before noon the Somerset House Inn— already one of Provincetown's most photographed houses—was ready for its special day.

In Natalie's room at the front of the house on the second floor, Peter stood beside the open window. The room was decorated in a safari motif and had a plush red velvet settee at the foot of the bed. This afternoon the seat was covered with bows, ribbons and Scotch tape, along with other colorful items from the eighteen-gallon storage box in which Natalie kept her party supplies. Natalie was renowned for her work with a glue gun and could bedazzle like nobody's business. She'd made Brian and Jason's wedding invitations herself, as well as the paper she used to wrap their handmade wedding gift, a black and ivory photo album with their names and wedding date written in calligraphy on the cover.

The only other place to sit in the room was the queen-sized bed, where Natalie sat cross-legged in the center of the zebra-print bedspread, her laptop propped in front of her on two pillows. Natalie's hair and makeup were done, but she still wore the white terry-cloth bathrobe provided by the inn. Her dress hung in a garment bag on the back of the bathroom door. It was Saturday, and last night had been cool, as early fall evenings on Cape Cod often were. But today there was no forecast of rain, and the sun was shining through the wooden window blinds. Peter felt comfortable dressed in his dark navy-blue suit.

"Don't romanticize the couple's relationship," Natalie read aloud as she typed. Natalie had decided they would start the blog with a list of things a single wedding guest should never do. "The couple getting married is not perfect, and chances are their marriage won't be either. Remember, pedestals are meant for floral arrangements and artwork, not people."

Peter didn't think Brian and Jason were perfect, but he found it hard not to romanticize the grooms-to-be. Brian and Jason had met ten years ago in Provincetown, when they'd been vacationing at the same guesthouse. Their first romantic weekend had ended with a ferry ride home to Boston hand in hand, where they soon became inseparable. Those closest to the new couple—including Natalie, Jason's sister, and Peter, Brian's best friend—thought they were a perfect match. As hard as he tried now, Peter couldn't remember ever seeing them fight.

"Oh, they fight," Natalie said, when he shared his doubt with her. "They're just very WASPy about it, all smiles in public until they're behind closed doors. Then they tear each other's pearls off."

Peter smiled, but he wasn't convinced. Brian and Jason had wanted to be married at the Dashwood Inn, the guesthouse on the East End of Provincetown where they'd met. But the long-time owners had sold the inn last year, and the Dashwood Inn was now a private residence. Peter wasn't surprised when he learned that Brian and Jason had taken a walk to the house after they arrived in town yesterday afternoon and rung the bell. They said the new owners were very nice, and now Brian and Jason were at the house with their wedding photographer, having their picture taken in the garden where they first saw each other. *How do I not romanticize something as romantic as that?* Peter thought.

"But you're right," Natalie said. "Jason and Brian don't argue often. Ten years later and they're still holding hands, even in front of my parents."

Peter knew what she meant. He could envision Brian and Jason now, sitting together on their sofa in their condo off Tremont Street. Jason always sat to Brian's right, with his legs curled underneath him and Brian's arm across his shoulders. When he visited their home, Peter would sit in the club chair across from them and marvel at their oneness, never having the sense that he was invading their space. Natalie was a frequent visitor as well and seemed to share Peter's feelings.

"They've never made me feel like the third wheel," she said. "I love them for that."

Me, too, Peter thought.

"Okay, what's next?" Natalie asked, returning her attention to the computer. She didn't wait for Peter to answer. "Don't just sit there alone," she read as she typed. "Get up and dance! Weddings are great opportunities to meet other eligible singles." Then Natalie laughed. "Except for this one."

Of the twenty guests attending Brian and Jason's wedding, only Peter and Natalie were single, a fact made all the more obvious by their prominent roles of Best Man and Maid of Honor.

"No more wedding parties!" Natalie reached for her glass of champagne. "That's what I told my girlfriend Laurie after she got married last year. I'm officially retired!"

Brian and Jason had sent a bottle of Veuve Clicquot to all of their guests in their rooms as a welcome gift. When he came to her room, Natalie had met Peter at the door with two glasses and an open bottle.

Natalie thought the blog should have pictures, and she planned to feature shots from all the weddings she'd been in. "Have you seen the movie *27 Dresses*?" she asked Peter. "I could have written it. But my movie would be called *33 Dresses, One Sari and a Woman's Tuxedo*. What can I do? Jason's my baby brother. I had to come out of retirement for this one. Always the bridesmaid, never the bride!"

Natalie took a big gulp of champagne. "Do you know where that expression comes from? I read online that it became popular in the Twenties, when the makers of Listerine first used it in an ad campaign. Can you believe that? A mouthwash ad!"

So that's it, Peter thought, looking down at his left hand. *If I can't get a ring on my finger, maybe I have my stinking breath to blame.*

He was almost forty and still had no idea how to find Mr. Right. On his dresser in his bedroom at home was a picture taken of him when he was three years old. His grandmother had kept the picture in her living room until she died last year, displayed in a silver frame. The boy in the photo had rosy cheeks, a dimpled chin and a camera-ready smile. *There are no guarantees in this world,* Peter reminded himself. *But who would have thought that boy wouldn't find love?*

"Check your past at the door," Natalie said now, typing at an impressive speed given how much champagne she'd drunk. "No one will want to slow dance with you to a Michael Bublé song if the ghost of your ex-boyfriend or girlfriend keeps cutting in."

Since coming out at age twenty-five, Peter had had three boyfriends: Joseph, a waiter at a steakhouse; Tom, a freelance graphic artist with a studio loft; and Michael, a travel agent. All three relationships ended badly. Joseph had wanted an open relationship; Tom had wanted to be with someone more "artistic"; and Michael had just wanted to get high. Though Peter didn't hate any of them, he'd seen them all naked, and couldn't stop seeing them in his mind, sleeping in his bed beside him. *I don't understand how some people can stay friends after breaking up,* he thought. *When it's over, it's over.*

Six months ago he'd met a man online named Matthew. Matt was a forty-five-year-old special education teacher with a great sense of humor, a cute cocker spaniel named Chloe, and an impressive cookbook collection. Matthew was crazy about Peter, and Peter told himself he was crazy. This was everything he wanted, wasn't it? Everything and more?

Matthew is a lovely man. A lovely man I don't love.

Last weekend he'd tried to send Matthew a message, to tell him again how sorry he was. But Matt had already unfriended him on Facebook. *When it's over, it's over.*

"My niece Emma turned six last month," Peter said. "I love both my nieces and nephew, but Emma... From the time she was little, maybe a year old, I remember whenever I came into a room, her face would light up with this huge smile. She'd immediately stop playing with whatever toy was in front of her and put her hands over her head. Emma wanted *me* to hold her. She's so smart and so beautiful—there's nothing I wouldn't do for her.

"Last year at Thanksgiving we were at my sister's house and Emma was sitting across from me at the dinner table, when she suddenly stopped eating and looked up at me. 'Uncle Peter,' she said, 'where's your boyfriend?' My sister and her husband are both social workers, both super liberal. Emma probably knows more gay people than I do. In that moment I could see she was putting it all together in her head, and something just wasn't right. If gay means a boy can have a boyfriend, and Uncle Peter is gay, then where is Uncle Peter's boyfriend?"

Peter smoothed the new tie he'd bought at Macy's especially for the wedding.

"I told Emma I didn't have a boyfriend. She stared at me for a moment. 'Oh,' she finally said. I've never felt like such a disappointment. I'm a bad gay."

Peter looked at Natalie. She was staring at the screen on her laptop, breaking the silence left in the room at the conclusion of his story with intermittent bursts of one-fingered keyboard tapping. Peter thought she hadn't been listening to him, and was about to accuse her of such, when Natalie looked up and held his gaze, as if to say *I've heard every word.*

"You remember Jeffrey, right?" she asked.

Peter nodded. Of course he did. According to Natalie's mother, Jeffrey was the reason her daughter had never married, was the "bastard who stole her youth." Jeffrey was a security guard who, in the twelve years he and Natalie were together, spent more time suing former employers for alleged workplace injuries than he ever did guarding anything. Then last September, one of Jeffrey's lawsuits was settled out of court, and the windfall was larger than anyone expected. The next month at her forty-fifth birthday party, Natalie was sure she would finally get a ring. Instead, Jeffrey had given her a waffle maker.

"After we broke up, I was a wreck. I didn't eat. I didn't bathe. I cried so much I thought I fractured my tear ducts. When shrinks are involved," she said, pointing her finger at Peter, "that's how you know it's real love.

"There were so many unanswered messages on my phone that my mother was ready to call nine-one-one. I finally dragged myself out of bed to my computer to check my email. I was so sure Jeffrey was going to propose to me that I'd bookmarked a bunch of wedding sites, you know, for decorating ideas. While I was deleting them all, I stumbled across an article about Princess Diana's wedding gown. Then I started crying all over again. Did you watch the wedding?"

"What wedding?" Peter asked.

"The Royal Wedding of Princess Diana and Prince Charles."

Peter shook his head.

"Well I did. July 29, 1981. I was fifteen years old. I set my alarm for five that morning so I wouldn't miss any of it. I know it didn't end well for Diana, but that day she was Cinderella. When she stepped out of her coach at St. Paul's Cathedral, it was like watching a fairytale come to life.

"So I'm sitting there at my computer reading the article about Diana's dress, when my eyes nearly pop out of my head. I couldn't believe it! Diana's wedding gown was here, in the United States. In Connecticut at the Foxwoods Casino. I could see it in person! That afternoon I threw out all of Jeffrey's pictures and took a shower.

"The next morning I called in sick to work and drove to Foxwoods. The line was out the door when I got there, but I didn't care. I was just happy to get a ticket. To kill time, I bought a souvenir catalog and was standing there reading it when I noticed this little girl in front of me. She was four or five, and she was standing in line with her parents. I realized that she was staring at me.

"I didn't know what she was looking at. So I smiled and asked her if she was excited to see the princess's dress. But the kid said nothing. Not a word. She just kept staring at me. I started to wonder if there was something wrong with her.

"Then the line started moving, and before long we were inside. The kid's parents pulled her toward Diana's tiaras. I headed straight for the Wedding Gallery. And suddenly there it was.

"It took my breath away, it was so beautiful. Ivory silk taffeta, antique lace, the twenty-five-foot train. This was one of the most famous dresses ever made, worn by one of the most famous women who ever lived. And I was standing in front of it! I looked at Diana's gown in the glass case and thought, *You're going to be all right.*

"Then all of sudden, I see her! The kid! Staring at me from the other side of the display case! I stare back and I'm ready to scream *What the hell do you want?* when the kid says in a voice loud enough for Diana to hear all the way back in her grave in Althorp, 'YOU DON'T HAVE A HUSBAND!'

"That was the moment I realized something I'd suspected all along was true," Natalie said. "Children are assholes."

There were voices and laughter coming from downstairs, and they heard Brian and Jason returning to the inn.

"That sounds like our cue," Peter said.

Natalie swallowed the last of her champagne and closed her laptop. "To be continued!"

Peter left Natalie to finish dressing and went downstairs, thinking she'd chosen the wrong title for her blog. *The question isn't how to be single at a wedding,* he thought, *but how to forget you are.*

The night before, Natalie had tried to forget by throwing a welcome party for the wedding guests and busying herself with crab cakes, baked clams, and wines from a vineyard in Truro. Tonight, Peter would try to forget by losing himself in the crowd of men outside Spiritus Pizza after the bars had closed, and perhaps—if the gods were feeling generous—watching the sunrise from a bed other than his own.

Across from the Somerset House Inn on Commercial Street, tourists and passersby had stopped outside a coffee shop to watch the ceremony. Some were taking pictures with their cell phones. The guests had gathered in the garden and stood facing the porch, where the exchange of vows would take place.

Cocktails and hors d'oeuvres would be served in the Somerset's main room immediately following the ceremony, a wedding gift from the innkeepers. Afterward, the grooms and their guests would walk five blocks up Commercial Street, past East

End shops and art galleries, to the waterfront restaurant where a private dinner for twenty-two had been arranged.

There was no mistaking who was getting married. Brian and Jason were dressed in identical black tuxedos, with matching white dress shirts and silver cuff links, shiny black patent-leather shoes, and perfect black bow ties the grooms had tied themselves. *"We two boys together clinging,"* Peter thought, recalling his favorite Whitman poem when he saw them standing together beside the fireplace. *"Fulfilling our foray."*

The grooms were talking with the Justice of the Peace as Peter stepped into the room. Brian winked at Peter when he saw him. The Justice of the Peace was a middle-aged man who worked in the Town Hall. Today he was dressed in a black suit, but each August at the Carnival Parade he made an annual appearance as his alter ego, Provincetown radio DJ Lady Di. Peter was wondering if Natalie knew the justice's ironic backstory when they heard the sound of her heels coming down the hall.

"Hello, boys."

She wore a sleeveless silk dress in gorgeous burnt orange, with an A-line skirt that fell just below the knee. Her pashmina shawl was chocolate brown, as was her vintage purse and suede peep-toe pumps.

Natalie kissed her soon-to-be brother-in-law, and then her brother, who presented her with a bouquet of yellow roses.

"You're beautiful," Peter said.

"So are you. And you're not a bad gay." Natalie kissed him on the cheek. "You're my gay."

The Justice of the Peace signaled that it was time for the ceremony to begin. Peter checked the front pockets of his suit pants. Brian's ring was in his right pocket, Jason's in his left. Natalie took Peter's arm and they stepped onto the porch.

Peter took his place beside Brian, on his left, and Natalie

stood next to Jason on his right. Behind him, Peter could hear Jason and Natalie's mother crying softly in the garden. He glanced past the grooms and looked at Natalie, his hands flat at his sides, covering the two rings.

I hope she finds her own best man.
I hope I do, too.
I do, I do.

THREE THINGS
I PRAY

Trebor Healey

The Archangel Michael, Who Battles Dark Forces
A real Romeo that angel was. And what better place for it—
what with the balcony, the Italian ambience, the tragic air
permeating the grimy old glorious architecture. Buenos Aires
felt lost in time, Mediterranean, forgotten. The world and Evita
had left it in the past, stewing in debt and unrealized potential. The usual suspects: sex and fate and the arbitrary slings
and arrows of the gods, the IMF having been the most recent
that seduced, loved and then abandoned them like the Zeus
that Europe and America were, and always had been. Mount
Olympus was up there in the Northern Hemisphere, and they
were far down here...below.

Calling up. Real Romeos.

And I'm some blue-eyed, pale-skinned, wrong-gendered
Juliet.

I'd spent my severance pay from the circus on a plane ticket
south, taking an apartment on Callao and Corrientes in the

heart of the city, among the theaters, bookshops and all-night cafes. The palpable nostalgia of the place with its tango and old bow-tied waiters unnerved me, made me feel like a ghost.

Had I fallen from Olympic heights? Had Juliet's rickety porch finally given? Balconies fell into the streets all the time here, crushing pedestrians. Maybe I hadn't fallen, but just expired and this place was no longer earth but the underworld.

If it was, I'd say the dead have great coffee and they're rather handsome. And the rain comes in summer, warm and hard from big thunderheads. I liked sitting on the little balcony outside my tenth floor room to watch it fall over the city among flickering lights, honking taxis and running-for-cover shadows down below. My room faced west, so I could watch the big clouds rolling in from across the pampas having survived the long treacherous trek over the Andes, all the way from mysterious unknown Chile—and beyond there, Easter Island, where the big heads stared into the middle distance.

I slept fitfully. Callao is loud; the dead walk up and down it all night long shouting and singing—football songs and insults mostly: *hijo de puta, che boludo* and the national anthem. The cabs never cease honking, or the ambulances screeching, because no one gets out of their way—ever. The street dogs join in barking when the confusion reaches a tipping point, then hands are thrown in the air, and if one listens carefully, from among those shrugs and sighs is heard drifting up like Romeo's longing, the national forever-frustrated drawn-out ethos: *este pais.*

Pigeons roosted on my balcony, their characteristic flutter and low murmurs almost a comfort. Which is what I assumed woke me that morning: the telltale crash of wings against glass, the fluttering, the muffled high-pitched moan. Poor thing. They're tough, though. I figured it would be fine, thought no more of it and pulled the pillow over my head, hoping to steal a few more minutes of sleep before the bustle and noise of Callao woke me for good.

I mused languorously about the coffee I'd drink with *medi-alunas* or empanadas stuffed with Swiss chard and mozzarella as I drifted in and out of slumber. Soon I was falling headlong through the clouds of my subconscious, assailed by disturbing memories of the circus that then morphed into dreams of Juan Domingo and Evita Peron on the flying trapeze, Che clowning revolution below, chuckling and popping candied corn into his mouth.

But I was soon roused from my reverie by the taxis and ambulances crescendoing ten stories below.

I stumbled into the bathroom and flipped on the light, looking at my grizzled face in the mirror. *Growing old, dear,* I muttered before twisting the knob and climbing into the shower. I heard the flapping again when I emerged from the bathroom. I'd need to pull up the *persianas* (I didn't know what they were when I got here either, but they'd proved quite handy: wood blinds that you pull up and down over your windows to keep out the sun, the cold and the *ladrones*—thieves—that Buenos Aires was rife with these days). I grabbed the rope next to the *persianas* and pulled hand over hand because they weren't easy. But I stopped when they were halfway up because, to my surprise, what I saw instead of an injured or roosting pigeon was a very, very big bird. Huge white wings folded over each other in the corner of the deck against the railing. An eagle? A condor? I'd heard they had those in Patagonia. The animals were all strange and different here: *capybaras* and *guanacos,* buck-toothed little rat-like deer-ish things called *maras;* and *nandus,* ostrich-like birds that ran around the pampas. I hesitated. Not one of those birds I'd considered had white wings. Perhaps a swan had escaped from one of the many turn-of-

the-century parks reminiscent of the imperial cities of Europe.
Even the birds were lost in time here.

Whatever it was, it wasn't moving. I pulled on the cord slowly
to bring the *persianas* up farther without startling it. There was
still a window between us, so I felt safe.

My eyes bugged out when I noticed that under those wings
was a human head—with curly hair to boot, like some over-
grown cherub. *Ladron!* I concluded with a start, pulling the
opposing rope to get the *persianas* back down before the cat
burglar tried to get in. Imagine going to such lengths to rob a
tourist. Had he hang glided in or hopped down from the roof?
They were dramatic, these Argentines, from kids on the street
corner playing at *Maradona,* and that president who looked
and carried on like a soprano in some Italian opera, to those
nasty generals of thirty years past, who weren't satisfied with
just exterminating an entire generation—they had to disappear
them, steal their children and drop them from airplanes into the
vast Rio de la Plata, and then claim they knew nothing; had no
records.

I'd have to go down and tell the guard in the lobby. Though
I'd heard the *porteros* were as often as not on the take and in
cahoots with the cat burglars who sometimes went door to door
with them—after paying them a handsome cut of course—
robbing and bilking the very residents who paid for the now
colluding security so as to prevent just such a thing.

I heard the moan again. His ruse? It made sense if he thought
I was a tourist—a moan is understandable even to a foreigner
(no need for Spanish to comprehend that). Still, my curiosity
was insatiable and I tiptoed back to the window and stuck my
finger between two slats of the *persianas* to see if I could spy
him. He'd gotten up and turned around and was now looking
down off the deck, his naked back covered in blood where the

left wing attached—and indeed it attached: blood and carti-
lage and tissue were showing. These were either some amazing
special effects—maybe they were filming a movie?—or something stranger. I suddenly hoped I'd see a camera swing by on
a crane.

He turned then, like he'd sensed me watching, and when our
eyes met, I stumbled backward, letting go of the slats.

A friggin' angel? I didn't believe in such things. But those
eyes: intense, fiery, penetrating. Maybe *I* was dead, and he'd
come to remind me or carry me off to my hellish reward? I sat
on the floor on my butt, considering the situation. Anything
was possible. If it was a movie, he did need to get off the deck
and back to the crew. I could go downstairs and find out if they
were filming in the building.

Oh, what a cute butt he'd had when I viewed him peering
over the rail. It wasn't *just* that, either. Though I saw it only
out of the corner of my eye when he'd turned, it was downright
Roman, a real Caesar. He was incredibly hot is what it was, and
I felt aroused. Which was crazy: fright and lust didn't belong
together. Not that level of fright anyway. It was epic, awesome,
old world. Who was that character who'd turned into a swan?
Holy shit, that was Zeus himself! I hoped not. Because if he was
Zeus, that made me Ganymede. I fondled my grizzled graying
beard. I was no Ganymede.

I sat, trying to avoid panic. My curiosity piqued, I didn't want
to leave, but I was terrified to stay. Then again, I wasn't here on
vacation; hadn't come here to rest or tour. What did I have to
lose? I'd come here to die or be dead is the honest truth. I was at
the end of my rope—why not get on with it and explore the fray?
What's the worst that could happen? I'd get robbed or condemned
to eternal suffering. *Bring it on.* I got up and proceeded to the
persianas and pulled them up rapidly arm over arm.

I stood and stared. It looked at me with those transfixing eyes, and then it smiled. A smile I couldn't forget: kind and welcoming when I'd been expecting a cornered animal, angry and afraid; an arrogant skygod; or an avenging angel come to spirit me off to hell for my unrepentant sodomy. But those fiery eyes turned to the warmth of a glowing hearth the minute its smile emerged.

I smiled back, but soon its smile lessened and a tear ran down its cheek. It was injured, sure thing; I could see now that the blood from its wings spread all over its shoulder. I felt tears then, too, which unnerved me further. Its eyes seemed to direct my every emotion. I opened the glass door and fell to my knees. Which brought me face-to-face with Caesar (and render unto Caesar what is Caesar's). The emperor rose to meet me, entering me like the host.

What was I doing? I felt possessed, unable to tear myself away or reconsider the course I'd embarked upon. I saw strange flashes of light in my mind's eye; I heard people speaking Arabic or something; there was music and the scent of fruit. I muttered an Our Father and started in on the Hail Marys before I nearly choked.

I took a deep breath after Caesar had conquered me and returned to Rome, leaving behind his infinite legions. Then I looked up to meet the creature's eyes, which smiled again with that unbearable kindness. *What is it you want?* I implored softly, wiping the cum off my mouth and chin.

It moved its great wings slowly, winced at the pain.

I still had my doubts, but I was beginning to think he really was an angel, after those visions, his stupefying gaze and the bloody wings. But I didn't believe in such things. My mental health wasn't exactly stellar, I reminded myself, attempting to chalk up my visions to my usual paranoid fantasies. He was probably some artist or thrill seeker or pop culture icon filming some crappy movie. "You all right? You need help? Should I call an ambulance?" I stuttered in rudimentary Spanish: *Esta bien? Quiere ayuda? Una ambulancia?*

He shook his head with vigor.

"Are you an actor? A thief?"

He smiled again and shook his head slowly.

Well then. I didn't even have any Mercurochrome. I was an escapee, not a traveler. I remembered first aid cream in a little kit I'd thrown in my bag.

"Just a minute." At least this way I'd find out for sure if they were special effects.

I stepped inside and bent down to my backpack, rooting around in the side pockets for my first aid kit, keeping a wary eye over my shoulder for any shenanigans from the chimera. I wondered momentarily if I really were in fact dead. Maybe my plane had gone down over the Amazon and these last few days were the wanderings of my lost ghost, wholly ignorant of its own death. Sheesh—and then the angel sent for me couldn't get it right either and crashed?

I didn't care either way.

I returned to the deck and ministered to the chimera, angel, whatever he was, dabbing his wounds—which, I was convinced, were clearly real—with Neosporin and a clean white tube sock, assuring him I'd get more supplies at the *farmacia* just as soon as we used up the tube. I dabbed him with the sock and laid a towel across the bed for him to recline on, so he wouldn't bleed all over the divan. His wounds weren't deep; it was more or less a flesh wound, but messy, as it had pulled his wing away from his back and torn the surface flesh.

He lay back and rested, and I left him there, proceeding to the elevator, off to get more bandages and antiseptic.

Archangel Gabriel, the Messenger

I'd left Los Angeles when the circus went belly up outside Palm-dale. But I'd lost more than my dream job of clowning—I'd lost Anastacio, my lover. Like many of my compadres in the BubbleOpia Circus—or half of them anyway—he'd decided to stay in L.A. and hock his talents to the movie and TV studios. So it wasn't like we'd had a dramatic falling out or anything. We were just through and ready to go our separate ways. Or so I thought.

I'd been a clown for more than twenty years and had no illusions that I was suddenly going to be discovered by Holly-wood—even if I were, it would probably be as some clown psycho with a butcher knife. That wasn't for me. Stephen King and Pennywise had done terrible damage to clowning, and I resented them for it. Myself, I'd been a sad and friendly clown—someone you could trust—a hobo philosopher of a clown in the time-honored tradition of Emmet Kelly.

And my paramour, Anastacio, was a real player, which made me the put-upon, down on his luck clown even offstage. I could take no more of it. Set loose in Los Angeles, there was no telling the pain I'd be in for at his hands. Just his infidelity among the traveling troupe, and the numerous ostensibly non-gay Midwestern and Texas towns we'd performed in during those past two years, had been hard enough. The burning plain that was Los Angeles would make quick work of what was left of our love. I was through with clowning—romantically or otherwise.

Anastacio was a trapeze artist from Tamaulipas. He'd picked up with us when we'd played the fairgrounds outside Browns-ville, Texas. "Not a legal bone in my body," he'd told me when I'd voiced concern for his status and warned him about Kim Sook, the enforcer.

"He won't take chances with Mexicans; he just won't." He'd driven off a dozen of them: roustabouts, clowns, cage-cleaners and cowboys.

"My English is superb," Anastacio informed me.

"True that, Anastacio. But Sook likes to see proof. He's a stickler for the paperwork."

Anastacio put down his book on the Kabbalah. A bright little bastard, he was the fourteenth child of an old sorceress from a dusty pueblo south of Matamoros, and like anyone with such a mother and thirteen siblings to dote upon him, he'd been overindulged and praised for his beauty and brains. Since then he'd spent all his free time reading and fornicating. A regular Lucifer. He studied structural engineering, neurosurgery, animal husbandry, herbs, numerology, physics and necromancy, among other disciplines.

He'd grabbed my hand, told me I had a problematic destiny and that he was part of it. Then he laid out a tarot and pointed to card after card. "That's me, that's you, this is what happens next week": a confusion of swords and princes. He shuffled and threw another reading, peered at it and shrugged. "It always comes out that way for you and me."

"I don't go in much for the occult."

"You don't have to." And he kissed me long and lasciviously. We were divinely naked in no time. And repeatedly and frequently during all the following afternoons.

I'd had half a mind to harbor him in Nadine, the private trailer that I'd commandeered when Lucy the Elephant Lady ran off with a telemarketer in Baton Rouge. But I was always wary of Sook and his eagle eye. He'd been after me just last week for mooching postage stamps to send Christmas cards to my dozens of nephews and nieces, snapping with a scowl that I'd lose Nadine if I didn't keep my drawers clean. Consequently,

I reluctantly sent Anastacio packing after a mere five days of ecstatic gymnastics.

Not a week later, I was as surprised as anyone when I learned he'd been hired on among the acrobats.

How had he gotten by Sook? He must have gotten papers somewhere (it wasn't till later I'd learn he'd found Lucy's in my trailer, and after sacrificing a muskrat and mixing its blood with sage, he'd been able to erase all her information and put in his own). When I asked him about Sook, he said the dames of a nearby whorehouse had found favor with his substantial skills and beauty and adopted him, supplying birth certificate, social security card, and Texas ID.

The ladies would do that for him, charmer that he was. People lined up to do him favors. The boy had magnetism, and I didn't want to think how dark and winding the branches around that kind of beauty could grow. I didn't have to. Soon, half the circus was stuck on him. With his smile and his lithe brown acrobatic body, those big white Chiclet teeth and how he rolled his *R*'s. He stayed in Nadine a few nights each week and regaled me with pleasure, philandering only with women in the beginning. The Siamese twin girls wept in his arms and both swore their love; Betty the Buxom, with 56D cups, kept his cheeks rosy for three days running; the bearded lady shaved his pubes with her straight razor and diapered him as her own.

Meanwhile, stage left, Atlas and the lion tamer glowered in the way of lecherous men. Sure enough, when he got through the women, he turned to the main course and went man to man. First the roustabouts, then the cage-cleaners, ice-cream hawkers, popcorn concessionaires and finally the pole jockeys with their long sinewy arms.

But always he returned to me and Nadine. I prided myself on that, and I got the comeuppance for it, too. Became his fool.

He was as curious about bodies as he was about black and white magic and nuclear physics. After another blissful few days together, off he went again, taking up with Noah, the dwarf. Unlike the women, the men made me jealous. "He's thicker than you," he said cruelly when I'd asked what Noah had that I didn't.

"Why'd you move in with me if you love so many others? Just to torture me?"

"I liked your trailer."

Taken aback, my chin pressed back against my chest. "Is that all it is?"

He'd laughed then. "Don't be so melodramatic. You're my special one. We share destiny."

I looked at him suspiciously, the cad. "Can't it be just you and me then?"

"Destiny and monogamy? Are you crazy?" He laughed. "I'm a servant of larger forces."

Soon he disappeared for an entire week with Bennie and Adrian, the stilt walkers. *He'll ruin me,* I concluded. *Where do I sign?* I'd dream of us in midair. In waking he was acrobatic. We made love in the middle of headstands. I started taking yoga classes from the circus snake charmer to keep myself limber. To keep my Anastacio. My destiny intact.

Atlas was only a matter of time with his tattoos and muscles. A corny gay cliché.

As for myself, to keep my sanity, I pursued an erotic friendship with the bearded lady who told me, while she bathed me, that they'd threatened to cancel her contract if she ever showed up again in that black shift and pearls.

"You looked stunning." I shivered as she toweled me dry.

"I thought I was upgrading the friggin' circus. I bought it myself," she protested.

But Mr. Sook, he liked to keep things as is. If it ain't broke, don't fix it. Still, she hated the frilly Victorian dresses they insisted upon. And she hated Sook. Sook was the vice principal, the enforcer if you will. A former Baptist minister who'd fled Seoul when the congregation and the authorities got wise to his trafficking in young girls to finance the church, the Lexus and the country retreat.

"They fled. I fled. You'll flee one day, too," he'd defend himself angrily when the players muttered "pimp" under their breath.

He was right about that, if nothing else.

The big boss was Gil Webb, who I resented for how he made Sook do the dirty work while he enjoyed the chairman of the board routine, smiling and encouraging the players, handing out cheap compliments. He was an old carny with a gold tooth and a penchant for slugging Manischewitz, relishing the occasional knife fight when he came upon midnight intruders on the camp's perimeter.

He ran a tight ship with his first lieutenant Sook. It was said, in addition to the tooth, he had a heart of gold. But I'd never seen it. Not till the last day. And though I'd steered clear—I had no truck with him—he always paid on time and gave bonuses when the circus did better than expected. But on my last day, he paid me a fat severance, and looking in my eye, remarked: "You were the soul of this gig, Peaches. May the angels bless you." Then he spit out that tooth and handed it to me.

"That's very kind of you, Mr. Webb. I shall treasure this incisor."

"I just love me the circus," he'd enthused, staring into the night sky, his eyes glassy. "It's got me, it does."

"What'll you do now, Mr. Webb?"

He fixed me with a stare. "What won't I do?"

Last I heard, he'd been drinking steadily. They said he suffered from nostalgia. That he was from a long line of circus folk. Some said he was the bastard son of Emmett Kelly himself, and others that he'd escaped the Ozarks while just a boy, stowed away in the lion's cage, rationing off his beef jerky to keep the beast at bay through the long night and into Texas.

As it turned out, Atlas was a jealous lover and began to lay traps for me. Tiger cages left unlatched, parked kitty-corner to Nadine. I nearly lost my foot in a 'coon trap one Sunday on my way back from mass after Anastacio had wowed the choir with his a cappella rendering of "Ave Maria." Then Atlas put itching powder in my face cream. The crowd roared.

"Put a stop to it, Anastacio, or I'm bringing in Sook."

"A stop to what?"

"Bear traps, maxillofacial poison oak, the fallout from your philandering." I nearly raised an arm to him.

Out darted his tongue, and what followed was how he apologized and why he could do no wrong. He didn't leave Nadine then, except for shows, for three weeks running. Promised he'd be good. Even had two big midnight-blue angel's wings tattooed on his perfect brown back.

Atlas wailed after that in the alleyways between trailers. For weeks he moped about, despondent, drinking, and singing old gospel songs. But it was his giving lackluster performances that finally brought down the wrath of Sook. When the smoke cleared, Atlas was shacked up with a willowy lad of dubious majority whom Sook had commandeered from a local revival meeting.

After that, Anastacio moved on to the lion tamer. An insatiable hunger. Good place for him among those ravenous felines.

"You like nibbling on that little greasy moustache of his, do you?"

"You're my special one," he repeated, flipping the card off the top of the tarot: Wheel of Fortune. He put the bookmarker back in the *Gospel According to Ramakrishna* and pounced on me like a cat. I'd give him that. He was always upgrading his skills. A quick study, too.

Eventually he got a bad case of strep throat from one of his encounters at the truck stop east of Shreveport, and after oral sex I ended up with a prostate infection I couldn't shake. It would no sooner clear up than it would return with a vengeance. I felt like I was sitting on a stone, and sometimes when I peed I felt like someone was running a sharp knife along the inside of my urethra.

Doctors failed me, while Anastacio's efforts with meditation, herbs, affirmations, astrology and past life regression got me nowhere. He offered to take down one of the lions and offer him up. I told him in no uncertain terms that no creature should die for the relief of my glands. I learned to live with it. It came and went.

Love.

Once, soon after I'd arrived in Argentina, I'd gone to the province to meet a *curandera*. I could have done the same in L.A., but someone had told me this one worked with the legendary Gaucho Gil and I was encouraged. Gaucho Gil appealed to my clown's soul. A folk saint of a century ago, he was a regular Robin Hood and was credited with healing those near death. His little red shrines could be seen all along the highways, patron of travelers and thieves. Handsome, too, holding the bolas characteristic of gauchos. I can't have been the only one to think of his balls.

Across the dirt road where I waited in line at the *curandera*'s, a boy sat atop a wall, watching the people and stray dogs and peering into the far distance from his perch. Now and again his mother yelled up at him: "Get off that wall before you fall and hurt yourself!" He smiled nonchalantly and waved back toward the house, which I couldn't see as it was somewhere beyond the wall.

The old man in line behind me muttered and slurped his *mate*.

I was ushered in, and the *curandera* waved her hand over my name after she'd written it down: I'd need to sacrifice a goat. "Only blood will cure blood," she'd stated. Then she went on and on about her dog from when she was a girl, how she'd carried it hidden in a backpack to school as her mother wouldn't allow her to keep it in the house. It stayed quiet, as if it knew its life depended on it. "I never had another human friend after that," she said. "Do you have money?"

"For what?"

"The goat."

"How much?"

"Well, the chicken, the goat, the candles: two hundred pesos."

"I don't have that much. And I don't want to kill a goat or any other creature."

She shrugged. "You don't have to."

"Did you kill your dog?"

"No, dogs are here to teach us about love and loyalty."

"And goats?"

"They're here for different reasons. They're not teachers. They're here to serve."

"What about Gaucho Gil?"

"What about him?"

The kid was still there when I walked out. Still smiling.

"Who is that kid?" I asked the old man who was going in next.

The old man shook out his *mate* cup in the ditch and pointed to a Great Dane dog loping down the street among the trash. "That's his," he said and disappeared inside.

As it approached, its enormity became more apparent. Half horse it looked to me. The child cheered and called to it, and it ran to the wall and barked up at him. The boy had an uncanny resemblance to the angel I'd see later, with his curls and his good cheer. The dog was no Romeo.

The Archangel Raphael, Healer of Men

I nursed him back to health. It only took a day or two. Angels heal fast.

He told me that he'd come back to Argentina to drive off dark forces.

"I've got a dark force here inside." And I tucked my hand up under my groin.

That angel fucked me, wings flapping, and off flew the pain. No dead goat.

"Who says a spent penis ain't a dead goat? Where's your poetry?" he chided me. Then he tickled me, and wrestled and razzed me in Aramaic.

I wanted to thank him.

"You've thanked me. I love me a mortal." He winked and I swooned.

"Don't go," I pleaded.

He shrugged. *"Este pais."* And up went the *persianas.* He opened the sliding glass door and outspread his wings. My heart was ruined. It opened with his wings—too wide. I had to crawl to the rail. Where I spied him high in the sky heading toward the Casa Rosada.

I thought of the flying trapeze and what a clown he'd made of me, this angel. And oh how I missed and longed for Anastacio then. Terribly. I curled up in the same corner where I'd found the angel and I wept.

They devalued the peso the next day. The street filled with people. I almost thought they were celebrating as they banged their pots and pans with soupspoons. Then the banks all closed and windows began to break.

Only Evita could save them now, I lazily thought, watching it all from above. Eva had apparently promised she'd come back, though that was endlessly debated. But if there were angels about, why not her, too?

I watched from the balcony, looked for her. There were blondes, but none with magnetism or riding on a half shell. And then I saw the curly headed boy and the big loping horse-dog running through the crowd, and Gaucho Gil on a mount swinging his bolas in hot pursuit. The boy just laughed and dodged and eluded him through the teeming crowd.

Soon, clouds gathered and there was rain, and all among it white feathers. There was a murmur that slowly replaced the shouts then. And it wasn't *"Este pais."* They were whispering "Eva...Eva Maria."

The crowd grew more and more quiet; they stopped marching and rioting, and instead loitered. Night fell, and candles appeared, flickering. Then everyone went home.

In the street it looked like snow had fallen. Not a soul. Then the little boy, head a mass of curls, running and kicking his way through the down, the dog loping and barking behind him. I yelled down and he ignored me as he had his mother, laughing and smiling as was his wont.

I tried another tack. "It's me, Juliet!" I shouted.

His upturned face; the dog's, too. His smile. The rain began again then, this time among it tarot cards: swords and princes mostly. But I saw the Fool card, too, the Lovers and the Magician.

I fled.

Home to Los Angeles. North to Mount Olympus. Back to my Ganymede.

ON THESE SHEETS

Steven Reigns

'm glad you got new sheets," Timothy says when we walk into my bedroom. I'd told him of my purchase earlier, the relationship going on eight months and the conversation spilling into the mundane of what we've purchased. As I'm taking the linen-covered decorative pillows off and pulling down the light-brown-checked comforter, I ask him why he's glad. "You've been with other men on that old set." The dark red lips of his large Muppet mouth smile.

We slide our bodies into the high-thread-count envelope of cotton and I feel uneasy. I reach to turn out my nightstand lamp, he shimmies closer, and I'm not smiling. I can't place my finger on the issue but tuck my right hand under the pillow while I turn to my right side, move my knees up, and he follows as we spoon.

I only wanted to change the look of my bed, not its history. There was a time when, newly out at sixteen, I longed for storybook romance. Thought the fewer I'd been with, the stronger the love I deserved. The less men I touched, the deeper I'd be touched. It was as if kisses, love, and sex were limited quantities and I shouldn't use them up on men during meaningless encounters.

In my late thirties now, I no longer think that way. I like myself more than I did in the past. Timothy is the best relationship so far. Those men I shared my sheets with for a night, weeks, months, or just an hour, I'm thankful for. They are the men who slowly helped me shape and build my self; it wasn't just sexual skills they taught on queen-size fabric. Through them I learned more about communication and preference. I think about the landscape architect I took home in a hurried, desperate rush after last call at age twenty-seven. The terrain of his skin was covered with thatches and bushes of hair. Those black, springy, coarse curls I soon found attractive. I learned that what I always thought I wanted—the smooth, milk-white skin of youth—might not be the only thing that satisfies me.

Timothy's breathing behind me paces mine as he drifts to sleep. There's nothing that I could share with him I haven't shared with others, except for the present. I can't change my past, and I know promises of the future don't mean much. I want the present to be gift enough for him.

I start thinking of Timothy as selfish or possessive. I've never lied to him about the men before him, the endless hookups and dating horrors. I don't resent the men in his past, but there are only a few. The sheets on his bed, though light gray, could be the virginal white of a wedding dress.

I fidget, trying to get comfortable, thinking about the pillows our heads rest on. How many men have laid their heads on them? How many have bitten or screamed into them in ecstasy, and how many times have I dreamt or even cried over men on

them? This bed, my life, is saturated with memories and men
from the past.

I come to Timothy, like all lovers, offering experience, not
virginity or anything close to it. "Hey, babe?" I ask. He emits
the quick *"Hmm?"* of the sleepy. "Did it make you uncomfortable we were sleeping on sheets I used with others? Are you
thinking about it like a metaphysical energy thing? Like there's
energy enmeshed in the fabric?" His left arm is still around me,
chest to my back, and he quickly starts to laugh. I realize I'm in
my head again, overthinking. I know this laugh; he's never used
it to mock me. His humor is pure.

The first time I saw him, from across the room at my friend's
party, I noticed his prominent smile and how he was amused in
conversation with someone else. I knew I'd talk with him before
the end of the night. I didn't know he'd be in my bed all these
months later.

He calls out his toy name he uses to poke at me, knowing
how much I cringe at it. "Cuddles, they're sheets, not condoms.
It's okay if you used them with others."

I'm more serious late at night and more sensitive, not quick
to let go after having talked myself into the idea that his initial
statement was menacing.

"Then why did you say you were glad no one else has been
on these?" Eight months is long enough for him to realize I can
overthink. He responds alertly, as if he just had his first cup of
coffee.

"I like that the sheets are something only I get to experience with you. It's another building of life together. They're not
sacred, they're sheets, but we get to lay in them together."

He's so kind to me in moments like this. In past relationships I would have wanted to process with him, dialogue until
daylight. As if resolution comes with communication, not simply

the letting go. "Lie," I correct him, nudging my left elbow back toward him.

"I'll keep my honesty and only consider changing my grammar." His hairy chest moves slightly when he speaks, and I feel it rubbing my upper back.

I reply, "Fine. I'll keep both sets of sheets and you."

VICTORIA

Erik Orrantia

Eastern Foothills of the Sierra Madre, Jalisco

The lanky calf sucked eagerly at the bottle. She'd been separated from her mother a day after her birth and since then, would put her lips on anything resembling a teat, including a water hose draped over the corral fence, the nylon pull cord of the feed bin, and Daniel's fingers as he tried to replenish her empty bottle. The nearly symmetrical black spots on the animal's shoulders reminded him of their first calf, Victoria, who'd been born nearly twenty years before.

He looked at Victoria in her private pen, the one Osvaldo had insisted on building for her, their "first baby," he said, the sentimental *vaquero*. "Good morning, Victoria!" She stood as still as a statue, except for her jaw chewing, chewing, circular chewing, as it did all day, every day. Old heifer stopped producing and reproducing a decade ago, but Osvaldo wanted to keep her, like a shop owner's first piece of currency framed behind the cash register. Currency didn't cost to keep it there though. Nevertheless, Daniel couldn't deny that she'd grown on him, a fixed feature of the ranch. He shook his head, pulling his fingers from the calf's mouth and replacing them with a filled bottle of rehydrated milk product.

He surveyed the large, empty roofed corral adjacent to the separate pen. The sun had appeared over the mountains. Osvaldo would be herding the cows in soon for feeding and milking. Daniel spotted him on the far side of their five hectares, cutting tall, green grass with a scythe he swung as they had when the ranch was only half a hectare and the herd count wasn't forty, but four.

Damned tractor sat uselessly in the barn opposite the corral. Ten thousand pesos for a new tire and a used radiator! Daniel had balked at the cost of the thing in the first place, preferring to trust a sturdy pair of stallions to a gas-guzzling green machine. Osvaldo pushed for modernizing, keeping up with the industry.

Swing that scythe, Osvaldo el Ranchero! The man's black hair may have been overrun by white, but his physique hadn't changed a bit, that Daniel could remember. Osvaldo's torso rotated with the agility of a young man's, and then he stooped to gather the cut blades and load them onto a cart. It was humorous. And sexy.

The sound of flowing liquid stopped. As soon as Daniel pulled the second empty bottle from the calf's mouth, she immediately began to search for more. "Not till later," he said, pointing his index finger at her face and withdrawing it before it got caught in her suction again.

He moved the water hose out of her reach before turning open the valve to fill the trough of the main corral. He left the water running and stomped to the house, chicks and chickens scurrying to either side, as if opening a path for him.

Inside, he stepped out of his boots, leaving them near the doorway. He grabbed a pitcher of pineapple juice from the refrigerator and set it on the kitchen table, flies lifting off from their momentary landing spots and returning to orbits in the kitchen. Beside an empty tequila bottle sat a stack of papers: bills from the grain supplier, Osvaldo's magazines, copy of a notification from Osvaldo's sister's lawyers—damned big-city bureaucrats—and last week's newspaper.

Osvaldo had asked him to take a look at it. He hadn't gotten around to it. He sat down and lifted his socked feet onto another chair, checking the tequila bottle for any last drops. He sighed and leaned his head against the wall, tilting his sombrero over his face.

"Did you read it yet?" Osvaldo startled Daniel awake. He hadn't heard the door open.

He pushed his sombrero up. "Ah, yeah. Well, what you said, right? They want to take away your sister's house. Her husband—common-law husband—didn't leave a will. No rights, right? *Common law* don't mean nothin'."

"I'm not talkin' about my sister. I'm talkin' about the newspaper article."

"Ah. No. Didn't get to it yet. Too busy." Daniel started to shuffle through the papers on the table.

"I saw how busy you were, Dani."

"Just a little siesta before feeding time."

Osvaldo stepped to the table and slid the newspaper from the bottom of the stack. He plopped it in front of Daniel: *Federal District Same-Sex Marriage Protected Throughout México.*

The gay marriage thing. Osvaldo and his crazy ideas. "Sorry. I haven't read it. Good for them, I guess." He scanned down to the picture of two light-skinned guys in matching suits with flowers stuck to their lapels. Their smiles were bright, bringing out deep dimples in one man's cheeks.

"Good for them?"

"Yeah. Let them do what they want. To each his own."

"Quit playin' so ignorant. You know what I'm talkin' about."

"What's the point, Aldo? We've been here for twenty years. We've got more important things to do than go running around in flowery coats."

"Exactly the point—you ain't a youngster anymore, and neither am I. You never know what could happen. Look what's goin' on with my sister. They want to take it all from her. 'She never was no good for him,' they said. 'She's the reason he's dead.' Now they want to leave her with nothin'! I told her to get married, but he didn't want to, and now what's she gonna do?"

Gay marriage? Daniel could hardly think the words without feeling a little queasy. *Gay.* What would people think? They'd lived plenty well in a big house with enough bedrooms to maintain the townspeople's doubt. *Gay.* All he needed was for their picture to show up on the front page of the newspaper, a fresh sack of corn for the town rumor mill.

"It's not that big a deal. It's a piece of paper," Osvaldo said.

Daniel stood and walked into the pantry, returning with a fresh bottle of tequila. He sighed as he peeled the plastic seal from the top, setting the trash on top of the newspaper. "If it's no big deal, just a piece of paper, then there's no good reason for it. Who's gonna try and take the ranch away, my old mother, my drunken brother? Anyhow, we ain't got no one who can run the ranch for us while we're gone." He walked away, looking down at the bottle and at the floor. Anywhere but at Osvaldo.

* * *

After a drink or two, Daniel spent the rest of the day completing his laborious routine by himself. He paired the bulls and cows that were ready for breeding, prepared milk cans for pick-up, cleaned out screens to strain the *queso fresco* and fed the herd their daily portions. When his stomach started rumbling in the early afternoon, he stood at the driver's door of his truck and gave the ranch a cursory inspection. Osvaldo was nowhere to be seen, as part of Daniel had hoped, so he drove into town for a roadside meal of succulent tongue tacos, the meat slowly steamed beneath a plastic cover, stuffed into handmade tortillas and slathered with spicy red salsa, chopped onions and fresh cilantro. A dash of salt and a squeeze of lemon were the final touches for one of his favorite meals.

Familiar ranchers and ranch hands tipped their sombreros to him as they gathered around the shaded taco stand, not unlike the cattle in the corral at feeding time. They stood and ate in silence, except for the frequent orders: "Give me one more, Marco," before the chopping began, or, "One Coca-Cola."

Most of the guys had been eating there for years. They talked at times—too much rain, or too little, rising feed prices, falling milk prices. Today there was little to say, yet there was a silent respect among *vaqueros*, and little need for words. Would the same respect be there if they knew, or if what they might suspect became confirmed? Would the tacos be served with the same casual confidence as always? Would the sombreros still be tipped?

After dusk, Daniel lay back on the twin bed in the farthest bedroom. He didn't mean to steal away, though he did close the door behind him, but only, he reasoned, because the radio had clearer reception in this part of the house, and a closed door made for better resonance. He looked up at the white ceiling, hypnotizing himself with the spinning blades of the ceiling fan. He lifted his head to take a sip of tequila from a glass he clutched in his right hand. *Gay marriage.* He could hardly fathom it. What was the purpose after all these years?

He reached over to turn up the volume on the radio and lose himself in *banda* music, tubas doling out the bass of old-time *rancheras,* and whiny voices singing *baladas* of broken hearts. When the tempo of the *tambora* drums picked up for a string of *cumbias*, the sound transported Daniel to a time when music and fun seemed to be the only priority. How he used to dance all night with family and neighborhood friends at weddings and *quinceañeras* and graduation parties. He hadn't danced since...since he'd stopped dating women so many years before. He let out a nostalgic sigh.

The door opened. Osvaldo glared at him. He walked directly to the radio and turned the volume down to almost zero.

"Where were you? Where'd you go?"

Daniel shrugged. "Got hungry."

"My sister called. She's going to have to move in with my brother in Guadalajara." He tightened his jaw. "I'm telling you..."

Daniel shrugged again, taking another sip of tequila. "There's nothing we can do about it." He reached over to the radio, conveying his annoyance with the exaggerated effort it took him to turn it up again.

"You staying in this room tonight?" Osvaldo said over the music.

Another indifferent shrug.

Osvaldo stormed out and slammed the door behind him.

✳ ✳ ✳

The shriek of a bird woke Daniel. He removed his sombrero from his face, surprised by the darkness of the night, nearly as black as the inside of his hat. He stretched his neck that had been kinked by his awkward position on the tiny bed. He spread his arm out to his left, noticing the emptiness beside him. The wearing off of the alcohol let guilt creep in.

He'd come to the farthest bedroom to piss Osvaldo off, and he'd turned up the music to boot. It was off now, only the red LCD light illuminating dimly. Osvaldo must have come in to shut it off. He was a kind man, a generous one, both persistent and patient. He was smart; too smart. He deserved to be treated better. Daniel knew he'd been an ass.

He remembered the trigger. *Gay marriage*. He hoped this would blow over soon.

He sat up in the bed, swiveling to put his feet on the floor, and pushed himself up. He opened the door slowly to avoid the creak and padded his way down the length of the hallway. The bedroom door had been left open a few centimeters. He walked in quietly and stripped to his briefs. Then he gently lifted the covers of the bed and got in beside Osvaldo. He slid over to a spooning position, snaking his hand under Osvaldo's arm until it found its usual nest in his patch of chest hair. Osvaldo's coarse hand clutched his and brought it up momentarily to his lips for a kiss, demonstrating, once again, a *vaquero's* creed—mostly words ain't needed.

The killing happened sometime in the night, strangely noiseless. The two men rubbed their necks as they looked at the bloody mess of bones, guts, and cowhide in the calf pen. Cattle hadn't mooed, dogs hadn't barked, roosters hadn't squawked. It must have been a cougar that had come down from the hills for an easy meal. The tracks were too big for coyote. The calf was only days old and defenseless, except for the fence of metal tubes that had surrounded it. The cat must have squeezed through for a leisurely feast.

"I'll get shovels," Osvaldo said, leaving Daniel where he stood over the carcass.

Daniel glanced at Victoria, who stared mindlessly in the light of dawn.

"Cougar?" he asked, raising his hands in inquiry.

She answered with nothing more than a blank face, as if saying, "What do you think, you idiot?"

He looked down at the calf's little face, recalling the way it so fervently consumed its milk the day before. Those black shoulder spots now stained red. He tried to grunt away a lump in his throat, and he wiped moisture from his eye, probably from sleepiness or an allergy. No, he had to admit he felt sadness. They sold cattle every week, knowing they'd be headed for the slaughterhouse. But this one, so young and innocent, so reminiscent of Victoria, and hence, symbolic of the start of their relationship and their hopes so long ago, had barely had the chance to breathe before she was brutally killed. What if their dreams had been snuffed out so easily? What if one of them lost his life so suddenly?

Out in the field, they dug quietly together and hauled what was left of the calf's body to a shallow grave. Later in the day, rain clouds added to the melancholy mood as they prepared *tortas* of pork leg, each man wordlessly assuming tasks complementary to the other's to prepare the sandwiches, before they finally sat at the table to eat.

Federal District Same-Sex Marriage Protected Throughout México. The newspaper article blared out at Daniel from the top of the stack of papers.

Hc bit a mouthful of *torta* and swallowed it down with a swig of cold beer. He remained pensive for a moment and finally looked Osvaldo in the eyes. "Who can take care of the ranch if we go?"

"Teodoro," Osvaldo answered instantly, not allowing even the slightest smile to form in the corner of his mouth.

"Okay. We tell people we're going for *business.*"

This time Osvaldo let a smile show. Daniel grinned, shaking his head. Osvaldo must have known he'd get his way sooner or later. He always did.

From the airplane, Mexico City was an expansive grid of blocks and blocks and blocks in perfect squares like grade-school graph paper. Daniel watched cars and buses moving between endless gray buildings, occasional roundabouts marking junctions of lengthy, straight roads like circles on dot-to-dot puzzles. Orange subway trains surfaced between tunnels, only to submerge again. The plane touched down with the jolt of a galloping horse jumping over a fallen log. He looked at Osvaldo, whose mouth fell open in wonderment. Daniel elbowed his arm to snap him out of his stupor.

They retrieved their sombreros from the overhead bin, the seatbacks having prohibited the *vaqueros* from wearing them. Daniel placed his black hat on his head where it belonged. He'd felt naked and awkward for the duration of the flight. The bustle of the airport astounded him, as men in suits and women in skirts pulled wheeled suitcases, and strangers of all colors and shapes walked briskly in every direction. Even sombrero-toting *vaqueros* didn't make eye contact or acknowledge their obvious commonality with so much as a nod.

After they'd waited in a lengthy line and paid an exorbitant sum for a taxi ticket through a thick glass window, a little green taxi delivered them to the economy hotel reserved for them by a girl at the travel agency/beauty-supply shop back home.

That evening, they ventured out, walking down the sidewalk of a busy thoroughfare. A steady rain began to fall and made the walk, already dangerous because of the uneven cracks and uncovered pits and raging traffic, a slippery endeavor for snake-skin boots. They returned to the hotel with wet plaid shirts and a soggy paper bag containing flavorless enchiladas and refried beans in Styrofoam boxes. Daniel couldn't wait to get it over with—sign the papers and return home to the green outdoors, the smell of fresh air and the cows, hearty food, and tequila. He'd imagined that the two would make an intimate experience of the evening. Instead, feeling so out of place, a goat in a rodeo, had drained him entirely of energy. He was asleep on one of the two hard beds before the end of the *"Chavo del Ocho"* rerun.

In the morning, orange sunlight entered between the blinds. Daniel felt rejuvenated. He turned toward Osvaldo in the other bed, listening to his lazy snores. He watched as Osvaldo's upper lip moved, and his moustache along with it, the moustache Osvaldo's sister had said was identical to his. Ignorant woman—the black tone of his was far darker than that of Osvaldo's. When the two men had met, only a few scraggly whiskers had populated Osvaldo's face. Now white hairs had begun to invade his facial hair, chest hair, even his pubes. Daniel smiled at the old man—still two years younger than himself—and found it hard to believe that those days had led them to this one, their wedding day. The thought made his heart beat fast with anxiety.

He folded the sheets back to get out of his bed and cross the gap to Osvaldo's. "Move over," he whispered.

"Hmm?" Osvaldo said groggily. "Did you fill the trough?"

"You're still dreaming. We're in Mexico City."

Osvaldo opened a single eye and stretched an arm out to receive him. "Come here, *cabrón*."

Daniel got into the little bed as well as he could, resting his head on Osvaldo's chest. His heart sounded as strong as ever.

"Today's the big day," Osvaldo said.

"Yeah. Friday."

"Don't be an imbecile." Osvaldo smiled, his eyes closed again. "You'll finally be a real man."

"If you say so." Daniel laughed, flicking Osvaldo's nipple with his tongue. He reached his hand down between Osvaldo's legs, anticipating the hardened state in which he'd find it. In that regard, Aldo never disappointed.

"You're crazy," Osvaldo said, pushing his hand away. "We're not supposed to till after the...*business*."

"That hasn't kept you for the past twenty years."

"It's keeping me today." Osvaldo smiled coyly. "Besides, I gotta go pee."

He got up and headed straight for the bathroom. Daniel heard the shower running and realized Osvaldo meant what he said. Perhaps he was right—better to wait. God may or may not have been around all their years together, but He'd likely show up at least for their wedding.

By late afternoon, they found the municipal palace, which reminded Daniel of its counterpart back home, only about thirty times larger. The colonial building of dark brown-bricks stretched an entire city block and stood three stories tall. Ornate concrete figures framed the doors and windows and dressed the roof. Considering the majestic appearance of the building's exterior, inside, the civil registry department looked dreary and disorganized. A long line of people, mostly couples, extended out the door into the hallway. Most men wore suits, their women in dresses. Daniel and Osvaldo had brought their newest blue jeans, their formal sombreros, and their best boots specially buffed two days prior by Osvaldo.

"Are you excited?" a young man in front of Daniel turned and said, taking Daniel by surprise.

Daniel looked at Osvaldo and back at the young man, whose hair was long on one side of his head and cropped short on the other. The young man clung desperately to another like an amateur rider to a bull. Daniel shrugged and tried to smile politely. "Sure. We're excited," he answered tepidly.

"Are you going to Zona Rosa after?"

"Um, yeah."

An hour later, a twiggy man wearing a fat tie and sitting behind the counter accepted their paperwork, checked their IDs and marriage permit, and quickly recited, "Do you each take the other in lawful commitment..." before he requested signatures, stamped the paper, and declared, "I pronounce you spouse and spouse."

Osvaldo took the paper from the apathetic runt and started to fold it like a letter.

"No," Daniel said, taking the document. "Let's not fold it." He opened it and read it, incredulous of the two names in bold black at the bottom, the signatures in blue and the imperfectly stamped government seal. His lips moved as if wanting to say something, and his hands cradled the parchment, a simple piece of white paper, yet as heavy to him as Victoria the cow.

Just down the hallway in an open courtyard, a girl behind a table sold pens and pencils, pads of paper and envelopes and other office supplies. Daniel picked up a simple brown frame and handed the girl a fifty-peso bill, waiting for his change and a plastic grocery store bag. He inserted the certificate into the frame and placed it in the bag, looking at Osvaldo with half an intention of kissing the man. It was their wedding after all, and besides, no one in Mexico City would even notice or ever see them again. But he refrained, limiting himself to a proud, unexpected smile and a knowing look shared between them.

"Where to?" the taxi driver asked, opening the door of the green Volkswagen.

Daniel shrugged.

"Zona Rosa," Osvaldo answered.

The day was slipping into dusk when their taxi stopped at the side of a traffic circle six lanes across. "Zona Rosa," the taxi driver said. "Paseo de la Reforma."

"Look," Osvaldo said, tapping his arm.

Daniel turned around to see, in the center of the traffic circle, a gigantic stone column surrounded by enormous bronze lions and great white statues of historic heroes in action stances. His eyes followed the vertical tower to its peak where a golden angel stood, gleaming in the twilight. Her wings spread wide and she held out a brilliant wreath. She was the Angel of Victory, the bearer of justice and peace. He'd heard of her, seen her in so many movies, and studied her in history class long ago. But standing before her, he'd never imagined the impact he would feel in her presence, as if she were personally christening them on their wedding day.

He stood reverently for a few minutes until Osvaldo finally broke the spell. "Aren't you hungry? Let's get something to eat."

They followed heavy foot traffic down alleys lined with trimmed hedges and sculpted trees. A couple of women with crew cuts passed them, walking hand in hand. A group of boys in tight pants and sweaters boasting brand names watched as they walked by. But Daniel was looking for food. He read the signs on restaurants—French cuisine, Italian, Chinese, and Thai. He wondered if they were still in Mexico. Osvaldo raised his eyebrows and turned away.

They walked a few blocks until they reached another busy, one-way boulevard.

"Well?" Osvaldo asked. "What do you want to eat?"

"I didn't see anything. Did you?"

Osvaldo shook his head in defeat. "More enchiladas and beans?"

Suddenly their noses perked up in unison where they stood on the busy street corner. They must have caught the same whiff of something familiar. They looked across the street and then at each other delightedly. *"Tacos al Vapor"* read hand-painted letters on the side of a street stand. Without a single word, they waited for the traffic signal and then dashed across the road. The smell was heavenly.

A dozen people stood at the counter, grazing from red or blue plastic plates covered with plastic bags. Propane lanterns on each of the corners lit the immediate area.

"What'll it be?" said a man behind a steam tray.

"What've you got?"

"Brain, eyes, snout, cheek, intestine braids, and tongue."

"Tongue," they answered.

"Everything on them?"

They nodded and watched the man peel the spotted skin from a generous chunk, chop the meat to pieces, and fill heated corn tortillas with it, then top them with cilantro, onion and salsa. They lost count of the tacos they consumed, satisfied with their wedding feast. They stifled burps, paid an approximate total and walked back to the heart of the Zona Rosa.

Passing more groups of girlish boys and boyish girls, Osvaldo said, "Back to the hotel?"

From down the block, the deep sound of a tuba reverberated through Daniel's ears along with the telltale clang of steel *tamboras*. He led Osvaldo closer so they could read the sign: NEW VAQUERO. He was drawn.

Far from the run-down cantina hidden behind solid, unidentified doors that Daniel had imagined of such places, the open doors welcomed passersby in from the street. Dangling lights illuminated the wooden floor and the many patrons, almost all of them men, who sat and stood around cocktail tables. Many men wore sombreros and cowboy boots, all wore denim and most had moustaches, beards or beer bellies. Daniel stared at them dumbfounded—they'd found their breed. Notably, however, there seemed to be an absence of embarrassment among the patrons as they talked and laughed in their little groups, a few holding hands in the open, and one macho couple in the corner groping and kissing for all to see.

"Welcome, *caballeros*," a middle-aged man with an apron said. "Come in. Have a seat."

They took a table near the middle of the bar, listening to the music and getting lost in the atmosphere. After a few beers, the place became more crowded. When the *cumbia* started, men instantly stood up from their chairs and occupied the space between the tables. Before they knew it, the entire floor was filled with pairs of men, shamelessly arm in arm, the leader's right hand at the other's waist, the follower's left hand on the leader's shoulder, their other hands clutched in midair in perfect *cumbia* form. The dancing couples gleefully swung and moved as well as the adolescents at any party Daniel had ever been to, some showing off with complicated moves and turns, others pulling each other close in intimate unity.

Daniel lifted the top of the plastic bag, peering inside to read the marriage certificate once again. Tomorrow they'd be back at the ranch, the cows and the small town. They'd greet Victoria, argue over the tractor and fortify the calf pen. Things would be back to normal. Yet something would never be the same—this new, albeit secret, connection between them, a quiet, concrete revolution. Married! Really married!

Daniel reclosed the bag. He reached his arm across the table, offering an open hand to Osvaldo. "So, husband," he said, "do you want to dance?"

NUDE BEACH

Paul Lisicky

Matthias wasn't the kind of guy who was usually taken with asses, but when he saw the man lay facedown on the striped towel beside him, he couldn't finish his sandwich. The ass was a confident ass, not an ostentatious ass. It didn't come about from squats and lunges in some health club. It was an ass that knew itself, that moved through the world seen and appreciated, and as Matthias dreamt of resting his face upon its dark divide, the man rolled over onto Matthias's towel as if they'd been sharing the same bed since college.

The dryness of the lips, the silly eyebrow tics, the looking downward and away... Where were the reactions Matthias usually felt around men, especially beautiful men? He'd always said that desire depended on one partner feeling more than the other. Desire insisted on discrepancy, he'd say. It fed on a *lack,* but maybe that perspective was just one more way he'd been protecting himself these last thirteen years.

They brushed sand from each other's shoulders. They got off

their towels. Matthias glanced down the empty beach, grabbed the man's hand with a grin that pretended to be devilish, and pulled that hand into the woods.

"Hey, you," said the man after they'd been at it for an hour.

"Hey, you," Matthias said, still trembling.

They looked into each other's eyes as it is said lovers do. They came back into their bones, their muscles, their separateness. They laughed with—was it wonder? Nerves? It hardly mattered that there were sand burrs on their feet or mosquito bites on their heads. In a little bit, their skin would burn with the serum of poison plants, but that pain would only help them remember their hour.

They walked side by side up the nude beach, voiceless, listening. The frondage crackled behind the dune line. On the other side of the trees someone was charcoaling meat. Matthias's eyes teared, smarted. The face of his ex flashed in the sky ahead of him. Breakup: he still couldn't even say the word aloud. Breakup! Say it. Sometimes he pictured himself as a house, his wiring, plumbing, plaster, siding and roof sold for crack. In the wake of the breakup, his ex had moved in with a new man on the other side of the bay. They'd set up one life together within days of the split, with no struggle apparent. They were seen at the local markets, talking about furniture and produce, hand in hand, faces serious. Meanwhile just the shell of Matthias remained, leaning to one side as the storms passed through the spaces where the windows used to be.

When the men reached the parking lot, the sky reddened above the tree line. They were back in the world. They'd stepped out of one kind of time into another, and this kind of time wanted something of them. Or they wanted something of time, which is always a scary thing, as time has its own plans for humans.

Still, none of that stopped Matthias from asking for the man's number.

"My phone's not with me," the man said. "But I have a business card." He slid off his backpack, dug around at the bottom with his hand. "Here. Text me later? Or you can call."

Matthias pocketed the card and with a kiss sent the man off into the night. The car crawled down the winding drive, brake lights pulsing before each speed bump as if the man inside had second thoughts about moving on.

He was the one. The man. He was the one he'd spend the rest of his life with. Because Matthias was certain of this, because he never felt this shudder of knowledge with the man he'd broken up with, Matthias decided to wait before thumbing the number into his phone. Once he got home, he walked into his kitchen and heated up a plate of lotus roots from the Chinese restaurant. He sat on the webbed chair, on his back deck, the soles of his feet burning with a rash. He looked up at the water tower. Was the man thinking about Matthias? Of course he was. He was thinking everything Matthias was thinking, which was why he wouldn't hurry up to send that text.

It didn't completely shock Matthias when the card wasn't in his pocket two days later. Clumsy Matthias! Surely, the card would turn up where he didn't expect it. He checked the pockets of his windbreaker, checked the inside of a novel and then another. He looked and looked in the same twenty places. He couldn't be that stupid—*Come on!* He thought more of himself than that. Just before he turned the lights off for the night, he turned an old suitcase upside down and shook it with a violence that startled a part of him. On the floor lay a picture of his ex, running up the street toward him, years back, eyes bright, face still ruddy with health.

Perhaps if he stopped trying so hard...

Matthias took part in these searching rituals four times a day over the next month. One Thursday, after he'd finished his shoulder shrugs at the gym, he drove out to the parking lot where he'd said good-bye to the man. He waited until he was completely alone, then got down on his hands and knees and felt the crushed stones. He imagined himself as a blind person. Maybe a blind person would have better intuition as to where lost things ended up. He pressed his face close to the ground. It smelled of mold, oil, vegetables, the pages of a book. He thought he would kiss it, and then he went ahead and did it. He wiped his mouth on the back of his fist, and then he kissed the stones again.

That night Matthias dreamt of the last night he'd spent with his ex. The night had been lovely. They'd run all the way to the beach and back, and they were just about to sit down to watch *Les Diaboliques,* their favorite movie. The ex put his arms around Matthias from behind. It would have been easier if the ex hadn't been so damn sexy about it, the hard ridge of his pelvis pressing into Matthias's ass—when was the last time he'd tried something like that? The ex took a breath to say that Matthias was a nice enough guy, and though it was very hard to say this, he hadn't wanted to touch him for years. In fact he'd never wanted to touch him, even though he loved him more often than not, especially when he was tending the cactus or scraping old paint off their porch. It had worn him down to keep pretending, as he was sure it had worn Matthias down. And would he like to meet the landscaper he'd been getting high with for the last seventeen months?

Matthias lingered in a chair in the coffee place one night. The couple to his left sat in silence, one face blazing with hurt, the other concentrating, folding a sheet of newspaper into something resembling a space station. The man with the hurt face

kept turning away from all the other men in the room. The
one with the space station kept pretending not to look over at
Matthias. They pushed back their chairs, stood. They punched
bare arms into the smooth sleeves of their jackets. Honestly, it
was a relief that they were moving on. They were distracting,
though they were nice enough to look at. And just when the
first man passed through the door, the second man looked over
at Matthias with a dark grin that said, *I want to fuck your
brains out.* And every time Matthias thought of that face, that
hungry face, it seemed okay that the card had escaped him. It
was almost enough to keep looking for it day after day. Then
looking for it some more.

TEA

Jeffrey Ricker

After her divorce, my mother didn't seem to know what to do with me. In the rush to jettison the faithless dead weight of my dad, it didn't occur to her that afterward she'd still have her son, a not-quite-eighteen-year-old high school senior, to incorporate into her plans, at least through the end of the summer, when I went off to college. It felt as if we were both waiting for our lives to begin. I was going to New Hampshire, where I'd been admitted to college on an academic scholarship. She was going to London, where she'd landed an embassy job and a two-bedroom flat with a tiny, green and light-filled kitchen where, four years later, during my summer vacation before graduate school, I found her crying over the dead boy I'd been sleeping with.

I didn't know that he'd died, and she didn't know that I'd been sleeping with him. What a stupid thing to call it, anyway: *sleeping with him*. Sleeping was never involved. Sometimes the bed wasn't either. (I hadn't decided yet whether my heart was involved.) I'd go to his parents' home late in the morning, we'd do the things we were sure we'd go to hell for, and then we'd go to the movies or the museums, shopping on Oxford Street for things we couldn't afford and didn't need. Sometimes we went to the pub. Some days, if there was time, we went back to his house and did it again.

I rested my hand on her shoulder. "What's wrong?"

"Oh, Mark." She looked up at me, surprised, as if she'd forgotten I was visiting. She wiped her eyes and waved a hand at her cell phone. "I've just had some bad news. Mary's son was killed in an accident."

She kept talking, but for some reason I couldn't hear it. Maybe there was a truck driving down the street. The window over the sink was open, and we could hear whole conversations when people walked past on the sidewalk below. That day, a Sunday, the street was empty; still, it sounded like the ocean filled my ears.

When I looked back, she was staring at me. She'd stopped crying, but her face was still wet.

"God, that's awful," I said. "You want me to make you a cup of tea?"

She looked down at the table and dabbed her nose. "Would you please?"

Tea was the answer to everything. Once a coffee drinker, when she moved to England, she left behind the bean in favor of the leaf. Now she drank a lot of tea and had a different blend for every need: English breakfast for fortification; Earl Grey or maybe a white tea when something delicate was called for; chamomile or green for illness; and iced orange pekoe with lemon to ward off the heat of summer.

I wasn't sure what the prescription was for tears.

I held the kettle under the faucet and stared out the window. It was starting to drizzle, drops spattering the warped panes. I shut the window; the rain made the glass appear to undulate, turning the world outside into a funhouse illusion.

I set the kettle on the counter and plugged it in. While it clicked and popped, I took down the ceramic teapot and opened the cupboard. The names on the tea tins read like stations on an East Asian railway I would never travel—Darjeeling, lapsang souchong, Ceylon, Assam, Yunnan, oolong. I looked again. There was no Earl Grey.

Shutting the cabinet, I turned to Mom. "Would you like to go to the pub and get a drink instead?"

She touched the napkin to her eyes one more time, then folded it and set it on the table in front of her.

"Let me get my purse."

Jeremy was nineteen, three years younger than me. Our mothers worked in the same embassy office. We met at a mixer for families of embassy staffers. My mom didn't like to schmooze, but she did enjoy a good gossip, so she wandered in search of the latest dish while I contemplated my Diet Coke and considered leaving early.

"Some of us are going to the pub later if you want to come," he said, taking me by surprise. I hadn't been introduced to anyone before my mom abandoned me—which sounds either pathetic or dramatic. I was twenty-two and an English major, naturally prone to dramatic statements. I hadn't spoken to anyone except the guy who'd poured my soda.

I looked at him a moment before I shrugged and said, "Sure."

At the pub, he said his name was Jeremy and told me about his parents (happily married), his major (music with an emphasis in vocal performance), and his boyfriend (he didn't have one, a fact he conveyed with a direct, unwavering gaze that left me somewhere between uncomfortable and excited). From there, we left the others to go to a gay dance club he'd heard about. After the first song he took off his shirt and tucked it in his belt. He was thin, solid but wispy at the same time, skin pulled taut over his frame as if life were barely contained beneath the surface.

I wouldn't let him take off my shirt—I was hairy, and soft in areas I'd rather not have been. Still, he unbuttoned my shirt, slipped his hands along bare skin and pulled me close.

He kissed me.

After about a year passed, he pulled away and looked up at me with that unwavering gaze. His eyes were green. He lowered his face to my chest for a moment—not sideways, with his cheek resting against me, but straight on, the tip of his nose touching the fuzz there. His breath was warm, and I was gone by that point. We danced a while longer then drifted off the dance floor and started making out.

It was a little after one by the time I walked him home. He slipped his fingers between mine for most of the way. Whenever no one else was around, he wheeled me around a corner, pinned me against the side of a building and kissed me with an urgency that intensified the closer we got to his parents' place.

"I'd ask you in," he said once we stood on the front step, "but I'm sure my parents are asleep by now."

"I want to see you again," I blurted, knowing that when I got home I wouldn't be able to sleep, especially if I didn't know when or if I'd see him after that.

"Come by tomorrow around ten. They'll be at work by then." He gave me one last kiss, pressing the whole of himself against me and leaving me feeling stricken. I stood for a moment on the step after he'd gone inside and shut the door. I wondered if there was some way to make the next nine hours pass faster.

* * *

I thought my mother would also be asleep when I came home, but she was sitting at the kitchen table drinking a cup of tea and reading a *Hello!* magazine.

"The kettle's still hot," she said.

"Thanks." I took down a mug and pulled a bag of chamomile out of the tin. My lips still tingled. I was sure she'd be able to smell him on me.

"Did you have fun tonight?" she asked. I sat down across from her and circled my mug with my hands, as if they were cold.

"Yeah, I met some nice people." My face felt hot. I couldn't have told her the names of anyone else at the mixer except Jeremy.

She flipped a page. "That's good. Maybe you'll have some people to go to museums with."

I didn't think my mother meant to sound uncaring. After everything she went through with my father, her empathy muscles seemed to contract. All of her did, sometimes. I'd look at her when she was sitting right in front of me and wonder where she'd gone.

The pub on the high street was popular with students. They were friendly enough, but rowdier than me. A couple of times I'd stopped in and felt like I'd stumbled into the locker room after a soccer match. Apart from that, the atmosphere wasn't memorable. The bartender was a bag of hammers, but even she wasn't enough to distinguish the place.

On a Sunday afternoon, it was quiet. The bag of hammers wasn't there; in her place was an older man, his face red and weathered, his sleeves pushed up to his elbows as he washed and dried glasses. He looked up when we walked in. I guessed from the warmth of his smile that he knew my mother. He frowned, though, once she took off her scarf and the sunglasses she wore even on cloudy days.

"Something the matter?" he asked. "You look like you're in a state."

She smiled in mock affront as she wound her scarf around her hand. "Thank you very much, Ray. I'll have the usual." She tucked the scarf in her purse. "What'll you have, dear?"

"Pint of Guinness, please," I said to the bartender. He nodded and put a glass under the tap and then got out a bottle of wine. I didn't know my mother had a usual drink besides tea, nor that she was at the pub often enough to be on a first-name basis with one of the bartenders.

"So what has you upset?" he asked.

"Oh." She fluffed her hair while his back was turned. At some point before we left the flat, she'd put on lipstick. "We had some bad news about a coworker of mine. Her son was killed today."

Ray sucked in air through clenched teeth, as if he'd sliced open a finger with the knife he was using to remove the foil from the wine bottle.

"Christ almighty," he said, "what awful news. How did it happen?"

"He was texting someone on his mobile and not watching where he was going." Her voice was tight with unshed tears. "He walked into a zebra crossing right in front of a car. Driver didn't have time to stop."

I nodded as Ray slid my pint in front of me. He nodded back, his formerly ruddy face now a bit pale. I didn't want to look in the mirror behind the bar to see if I'd gone similarly ashen. Jeremy and I had traded a couple of texts earlier that morning, making plans to meet tomorrow.

My mother pulled a ten from her purse, but Ray waved her

off. "This one's on me."

"Cheers," she said. She lifted her glass toward me and smiled sadly. "To the departed."

I clinked and felt Jeremy's name swelling in my throat, dying for me to say it out loud. Instead I took a long pull from my pint and kept quiet.

"I suppose they'll be leaving to do the funeral back home," she said, not to me or to Ray in particular. "It's all so sad, really."

"Texting," Ray said a little explosively, as if the word or the act of texting itself were a bomb. "Walking right into the street. What the devil was he thinking?"

I took a longer drink to quench my rising anger. Who the hell was he to pass judgment? He produced a box of tissues from underneath the bar and placed them near my mother's arm.

"Just in case," he said.

The mews cottage where Jeremy and his parents lived lay off a quiet road a few blocks from the high street. I got there before ten, so I walked around the block once, then twice. When I looked again at my watch, I was still ten minutes early. I walked down to the high street and back, trying to take each step as slowly as possible.

Jeremy opened the door before I knocked.

"I was wondering where you went," he said, smiling.

He wore a pair of jeans and a green T-shirt, no shoes. His hair still looked a little damp; he must have gotten out of the shower not long before.

"I saw you walk around the block and then head off. I was thinking you'd changed your mind."

"Oh," I said. I still stood on the doormat. He hadn't invited me in. "I was early."

"That's okay. They leave for work before nine, but I needed time to get ready." He grasped my hand and pulled me inside.

From the dim entryway he led me through an equally dark sitting room toward the back of the cottage where the kitchen fairly exploded with light from a sunporch with a tiny patio beyond, a private little shelter guarded by the backs of surrounding buildings. Houseplants cast the sunlight in a green glaze, momentarily rustled as a black and white cat leapt off the table and darted between us.

"Knock it off, Boris," Jeremy said. "Want something to drink?"

I said I'd have a glass of water—suddenly, I felt bone dry—and Jeremy told me to make myself comfortable in the living room. The dark space with its bland floral sofa and wallpaper felt worlds removed from the pints of beer and the pulse of music the night before. That morning, in that room, I could almost hear myself break into a sweat.

When Jeremy handed me the ice water, the glass already slick with condensation, it slipped right through my fingers. I caught it in my second fumbling effort, but not before most of its contents dumped on me. I groaned in frustration. At least I hadn't spilled it on him. Or the cat.

"Don't worry. It's just water," he said.

"I'm such a klutz."

"It's okay." He took my glass from my hand and set it on the coffee table, along with his own. Then he put a hand on either side of my face and drew me in for a kiss. He was less demanding this time, less desperate. It was almost gentle. Maybe it was the dim light of the room, but it felt as if we were teetering on the edge of dusk, not late morning.

He untucked my shirt and touched my belly, the skin there clammy and cold from the spilled water. I flinched.

"Relax," Jeremy said, his hands falling to my waist. He undid my belt, slowly. Taking both my hands, he pulled me up from the sofa. "Let's go upstairs."

Three or four steps up, I held back. His face when he turned to look at me showed no reticence. It was as if this had been the idea all along.

"It's just that..." I stammered. "I haven't done this that often."

He smiled and moved down a step until we were eye to eye. "Me neither."

Unlike the night before, when he began to lift my shirt over my head, I let him.

My mother and I were the only customers in the pub for a while. As our first round extended to a second, people drifted in singly or in pairs until it was fairly busy. To my surprise several of them knew my mother, asked what was the matter, offered to buy her a consoling drink. At that rate, she'd be drunk before supper.

Introductions were made, additional drinks knocked back, and my mother's mood immediately improved. She pointed out the woman who ran the bakery on the high street, and the estate agent who sold flats for more than I could imagine making in a single lifetime and who'd found my mother the one affordable flat in the neighborhood. I'd never known her to be this social, but maybe that changed after she left my dad. Judging from her new friends' treatment of her, she was still an amusing novelty to them, an amusement that I was a little relieved didn't extend to me. They were all somehow more posh than I was used to. We were not sophisticated people, my mother and I. I had no illusions about that. In any case, they were all much older than me.

Maybe that's why I didn't tell her about Jeremy. The gap

between my age and his was only three years, but it seemed like a much bigger chasm to bridge than the five years that had stood between her and my father. It was odd how much I had been the fumbling, bumbling beginner with Jeremy, though I'd had boyfriends (well, *a* boyfriend) before meeting him.

We'd made a complete mess of his bedroom before we heard the mantel clock downstairs strike noon. He bounced off the bed and walked over to the window. The room faced south, overlooking the kitchen and sunporch below. He flung open the curtains and stretched his arms over his head.

"Aren't you worried someone's going to see you?" I asked. He was still undressed. The view from where I lay was wonderful, the hard contours of his back lengthening into tight, long lines.

"Everyone's at work, probably," he said, "but even if they weren't, no. I'm not too worried." He turned around. "I'm starving. Want to go get lunch?"

I was already a little buzzed from my third pint of Guinness. Mom's face was flushed, which could have been the wine or the company. They'd talked her into going to a pasta bar a few streets over.

"Want to come, dear?" she asked.

"Actually," I said, "if you don't mind…"

"Oh, of course you don't," she said before I finished. I thought she looked a little relieved. "Why would you want to hang out with all of us dusty old folk?" She pulled a twenty out of her purse. "Why don't you pick up something at the store before they close? And if you could, get some Earl Grey. I think we're out."

At the entrance, her little entourage prepared to go left as I headed right toward the Tesco Express. She paused and turned back to me.

"Just don't text while you cross the street, dear."

My smile was more of a grimace. Had she just made a joke of Jeremy's death? Surely she wasn't that tipsy.

I watched them until they disappeared around a corner. I walked down the high street and paused outside the Tesco, looking in at the lone checker standing idly at one of the tills, before I decided to walk on.

At the end of the high street the road became one lane and veered right. If I walked straight ahead, the sidewalk led past a small park to an alley that emptied onto Baker Street. As I walked through, wind in the narrow opening whipped my hair and slapped an errant plastic bag against my jeans, where it stuck.

Plucking it between two fingers, I removed it from my leg—it was, grossly, a bit wet—then released it into the wind behind me. Freed, it went sailing down the alley and disappeared over the park fence. I wiped my fingers against my jeans next to the square of damp fabric where the bag had landed.

It was all so random, walking through the alley at just the right moment for the bag to collide with me. A couple of seconds either way, sooner or later, and the bag would have just been something I watched sail out before me or would never have noticed. If Jeremy had finished his text before or after getting to the zebra crossing, the car would have passed in front of him or behind him.

We'd had a close encounter with a plastic bag once. It was after lunch, which was after sex, but before we got to the National Portrait Gallery. We were walking along Charing Cross Road and Jeremy was writing a text. He didn't see the shopping bag drifting on the wind, heading right for his face. I reached out and grabbed it, dry and crinkly, before it could smack into him. Startled out of his concentration, Jeremy looked at it and laughed.

"I guess I should watch where I'm going," he said, and put his phone away.

"Did you hear about that girl who fell into an open manhole because she was texting and walking?"

"No." He sounded alarmed. "At least a plastic bag isn't fatal."

"Oh, she lived, but she felt really stupid afterward."

I let the plastic bag go, and we stood watching the path it took through the air.

"That's a metaphor, don't you think?" he asked. "Floating unpredictably through life. You never know whose face you're going to smack into."

I shrugged. I spent enough time finding symbolism in texts that I tried not to look for it in real life.

"One plastic bag," he sang, drawing out the last word so the note rose and fell in time with the bag's circuitous, tumbling course.

He kissed me then, right in the middle of the street, as oblivious to the gawking from passersby as I was aware of them. He pulled away.

"Hey, plastic bag," he said, his lips curling into a smile.

Night staked its claim on the city as I walked. I spent the better part of a couple of hours wandering along the perimeter of Regent's Park, down to Regent Street, and back up Oxford Street. The sidewalks were still crowded, though most of the shops were already closed. Eventually, I found another Tesco and stopped in to pick up Earl Grey right before they closed.

When I got home, my mother was at the kitchen table, once again reading *Hello!* Her face was a little flushed, but she seemed to be still on this side of sober.

"Did you have a nice dinner?" I asked.

She smiled. "It was lovely, yes."

I held up the bag. "I got more tea."

"Thank you, dear."

I sat down across from her, not sure why I didn't turn on the TV or head to my bedroom. I'd been here over two months. It was the middle of July. I had another three weeks before I had to be back at school. In all, I'd known Jeremy six weeks.

She kept paging through the magazine as she spoke to me. "Before I forget, I won't be home for dinner tomorrow. They're going to have a small memorial for Mary's son at the embassy chapel and I want to go."

"Okay."

"You'll be left to your own devices as far as getting something to eat, so—"

"Actually, I'd like to go, too, if you don't mind."

Her expression didn't change, but when she looked up from the magazine, she tilted her head. It was a way she had, like she was trying to see me straight on but out of the corner of her eye, as if that was the only way she could really see everything.

"Did you know him?" she asked.

Here it was, the why of it. Maybe I wouldn't be able to tell her the reasons I'd kept him from her. Maybe there wasn't a reason that could be put into words. I just nodded, and that slight movement dislodged something, like that plastic bag smacking against my leg suddenly let loose and floating away. I was crying before I could say anything else.

"Oh, dear." She reached across the table and placed her hand on my head. "I wish you'd told me."

I didn't lift my face, just nodded. She stood up and put her hand on my back.

"I'll make you some tea," she said.

A ROYAL MESS

Taylor McGrath

G raham stared wide-eyed at his computer screen. *My ex-boyfriend is working at the Federal Department of Parakeets? That can't be a real thing.* The people-search websites he'd paid for had turned up nothing for so long. He hesitated before clicking the link. Nearly all his friends had urged him to stop looking for Farrin, saying things from the ridiculous—*He was abducted by aliens*—to the possible—*His parents sent him to England.*

Graham had a journalist's insatiable curiosity, and it was three years to the day since he'd seen Farrin. There'd been one tantalizing post six months ago after what felt like eternal silence on Farrin's "Royal Mess" blog. And now this. He absolutely must click the site to solve this new mystery: Why the heck would the government waste taxpayers' money on a Department of Para—

Oh. It's a pet store.

How odd that Farrin's job wasn't somehow involved with

music. Maybe this was the only place that would hire him. That would be typical for Farrin, but with his troubles, holding down any job was progress.

Graham clicked a map. An electric thrill shot through him. If this was real, then Farrin was back from wherever he'd disappeared to, and his place of work was only half an hour away. Graham's Saturday plans for the gym and shopping evaporated. Now he needed a haircut.

Two hours later, he emerged from the Dupont Metro station still wondering why Farrin would choose a bird store. If Farrin was depressed about his life, was there anything encouraging Graham could say?

Birds are wonderful. You've always liked birds, right? Actually, didn't you have bird photos for all your security images?

But he couldn't remind Farrin of that mistake. The bad memory blossomed, and Graham stopped short. He could see the store's lettering and a cheerful green cartoon bird lit in neon. He shivered in the cold wind, turned around and fumbled with his cell phone. There was still one friend who remained patient with Graham whenever he brought up Farrin. He dialed.

"Tracy, I found out Farrin's back in town, and I'm going to where he works. This is a mistake, isn't it?"

He heard Tracy sigh before she said, "I don't know. He made you so sad."

Graham reflected. Tracy and he had become close only in the last year; she'd been friends with Farrin first. She'd always carefully walked a line between supporting him and staying loyal to Farrin.

He decided to be blunt. "The breakup was my fault."

There was a pause. "How so?"

"I was nosing around Farrin's computer; it led to our biggest fight. Really, our only fight."

Graham heard a voice in the background and recalled that Tracy had a new girlfriend. He should let her go.

"I'll make it quick. I saw his pay-phrase for his credit cards. It was 'Kabul Bombs the Bass.' He's Afghani. I'm allegedly an investigative journalist. I'm also an idiot."

"You can't be serious. Please tell me you didn't call the FBI or—"

"No! Nothing like that." Graham swallowed. "I apologized, like, thirty-five times. It's not like I got him on a no-fly list. I never told anyone."

Tracy said nothing. Graham paced counterclockwise around the fountain in Dupont Circle for warmth.

"I should've seen that's what made him worse. A month or so after that blowup, his depression was a twenty-four-hour thing. And his concentration? Worse than ever."

"Graham, Bomb the Bass is a music group. Also an expression, as in 'turn up the bass.' You know that, right?"

"I do, but I thought maybe there could be other implications—"

"The spelling should have been a hint."

"True, it should have been—"

"Farrin wanted to see his dad's city! He even wanted to be a DJ there. How could you not get that?"

Graham stopped twenty feet from the Metro and watched puffs of his breath. "I've got nothing. I won't bother him. Thanks for setting me—"

"Graham, wait. I'm sorry, too. I'm a DJ, so that connection comes faster for me."

Good point, thought Graham, as a portion of his guilt lifted.

"D.C.'s been the most paranoid place on earth for the last decade, and okay, Kabul and 'bass' makes me think of a military base, too. And maybe you don't know Farrin as well as

I thought. You know his family is Kashmiri, not Afghani, right? His dad grew up in Afghanistan in…exile or whatever. Then he had to move here. Farrin's never even been to Asia."

The word "Kashmiri" rang a distant bell, but Farrin had never talked about his parents or his background, which had made Graham more curious and frustrated.

"Exile? Why would his dad be exiled?"

The voice behind Tracy spoke up again. "Graham, if I don't go I'll be late for a plane. A gig in Miami."

"Hey, good luck!"

"And good luck to you with Farrin. I don't think his departure had anything to do with your mistake. Talking to him might help. He probably misses you, too."

Graham stood outside the bird shop, watching tiny finches hop from perch to perch. He shielded his face, more to hide his identity than to block the sun. What if the "transformation" Farrin talked about in that blog post from six months before wasn't all that real? What if he wasn't supposed to know about that blog post in the first place?

Don't be a stalker. Just go home.

He walked into the shop.

Farrin had filled out a bit and had a neatly trimmed goatee that made him look more masculine, and combined with his wavy black hair and long eyelashes, more sultry. He hadn't looked up when the door opened, saying only, "Let me know if you need help."

Graham took a deep breath as he watched Farrin feed an eyedropper of liquid to a white parakeet. The bird was surprisingly calm considering it was upside down and enclosed in Farrin's hand. Just seeing him and how healthy he looked lightened Graham's anxiety. The old urge to be silly in hopes of coaxing a laugh out of Farrin returned.

"Pardon me, sir. Do you have any big birds?"

Farrin still didn't look up. "Nothing larger than cockatiels. If you're thinking of something like a macaw or an Amazon parrot, I can refer you to a breeder."

"I was actually thinking of something for security purposes. Do you have any attack birds? A hawk? A large guard owl?"

There was a brief expression of *Oh? A wise guy, eh?* on Farrin's face. Then he lifted his gaze from the parakeet to look at Graham. His expression changed to surprise and thankfully, an excited smile.

"Graham! I didn't know you were in D.C.!"

"I didn't know you were back, either."

Farrin took quick steps to a cage and carefully placed the white bird inside. "There you go, baby." The bird situated, Farrin jogged around the counter for a hug. Graham's stomach tightened. Farrin wore a thick, soft sweater that Graham remembered by touch. He also wore the same citrus cologne that made Graham need to kiss his neck.

Dial it back, Graham.

Farrin went back around the counter and scribbled on a notepad. "So you live here again?"

"The suburbs. Alexandria."

"I'm back in Dupont Circle. I...uh, I'm sorry I didn't stay in touch."

A chubby boy bounded into the store followed by a tall, tired-looking woman.

"I want a blue one! A blue parakeet!" shouted the boy.

"Georgie, please don't jump and shout," said the woman. "You promised you'd be polite, remember? I'm sorry. My son's excited."

"It's my birthday! I want a blue one!" Georgie appeared to have the remnants of a chocolate bar on his face. As an image of Augustus Gloop combined with Veruca Salt crossed through Graham's head, he noticed that the parakeets and lovebirds in the cages nearest Georgie seemed agitated, if not frightened.

Farrin patted Georgie on the shoulder to calm him and knelt to look the boy in the eye. "But what if the bird who would love you the most and be the best friend to you is a green one?"

Georgie stood still, blinking several times in confusion. Then his face cleared. "I want a green one!"

The woman laughed, and Farrin's smile lit his brown eyes. Graham shivered. That was Farrin's second smile since he'd walked in. He used to smile so rarely.

Farrin raised a finger to Graham to indicate, *Hold on a sec,* then he began asking questions of the mother and Georgie. Was it likely they would get only one bird? Would Georgie have ample time to spend with a pet? Where in their home would the bird be kept? Were there other animals?

Graham raised an eyebrow. Did Farrin always interview customers to best match them with a feathered companion?

Graham caught sight of the notepad. He shouldn't read it, he knew. *But look at that. Farrin still has the penmanship of a first grader trying to write during an earthquake.* Graham had a lot of practice deciphering.

Good Things for February 3rd.
   Remembered to meditate last night
   Shower was actually hot this morning
   Guy down the hall told me, "Have a good day, hand-some."
   Bought a bagel for Friendly Homeless Guy
   Sold ~~three~~ four birds
   Grouchy seems better today
   Got to see Graham

* * *

Graham felt a brief thrill. He was a "good thing" for the day. But who was Grouchy? An ill-tempered boyfriend? Excessive willingness to put up with crap had been Farrin's biggest weakness. It used to make Graham so sad.

Graham studied Farrin as he explained to Georgie how to tell if a budgie was young and if it was a boy or a girl. He had an animation that Graham had never seen before, and a sense of alertness and contentment. Graham had expected just to see Farrin, hopefully get one of his warm hugs and then tell him he'd "see him soon," because if Farrin hadn't really changed, a long period together wouldn't help either of them. But Farrin's sweet and adorable side was evident, and the atmosphere of vulnerable gloom seemed entirely absent. Graham observed Farrin with his customers for ten minutes or more, and not once did Farrin apologize for being terrible at something.

Graham recalled the string of failures that Farrin seemed to "collect" when he needed to prove how incapable he was. He hadn't succeeded at being a disc jockey, playing clarinet professionally, learning composition for keyboards, finishing college or, according to Farrin, making his parents feel anything other than disappointment.

Now he made lists of good things?

Graham did a double take when Farrin had Georgie sign a "contract" promising to take good care of his new bird and to email Farrin with regular "budgie updates." The mother and Georgie beamed as they stepped past Graham with a large cage, an abundance of toys and a small cardboard box containing a green bird. Farrin told Georgie that the frightened budgie should be carried carefully, so Georgie tiptoed as if he held a cup of scalding coffee filled near to overflowing.

Farrin went back to work, calling over his shoulder as he

rushed around, "I'm leaving in about half an hour. Could you crash a wedding with me? First, I need to dance with some birds."

This was the Farrin he remembered: scattered, implausible, but most likely one hundred percent literal.

"Dance with some birds?" He followed Farrin to the back and watched him set up a small boom box. He noticed a yellow Post-it note that read, *Danger. Beware of Fussikeets and Grumpikeets.*

"These must be the attack birds I was asking about."

Farrin turned to Graham, smiling a third time. Again, the smile lit his eyes in a way that made Graham's chest tighten.

"These are mostly returned birds who may not have been treated well. They pull out their own feathers or seem unusually afraid of people, and they're likely to bite. They may never be companions to anyone again, but I want them to know they're still good birds."

"May I ask why we're crashing a wedding? Won't we be obvious in jeans?"

"It'll be fine. No one will see us."

Graham shook his head. It would probably be easier to wait and see what happened than to ask Farrin for details.

Graham watched Farrin thumb through music selections. "Yesterday we played 'Muskrat Love' for Darcy. Today is Grouchy's turn."

Graham felt relief. Grouchy wasn't a man.

"Grouchy's favorite song is 'Here Comes Your Man.'"

"What a coincidence considering that's also your favorite s—"

The bouncy, cheerful tune that had become the Pixies' signature hit began. Right away Graham knew which bird was Grouchy. A cockatiel in a cage by himself bopped his head up and down in time to the beat. Farrin stepped back and forth, mimicking the bird's movement on his perch.

Graham hid a smile. Farrin *did* have a job in music. He was a dance therapist for birds. But he noted that Farrin kept checking his watch. He seemed agitated and looked flushed.

As he was locking the shop, a thin, gray-haired man interrupted him. They had a rapid, irritated exchange in what Graham imagined was Kashmiri. The older man took keys out of his pocket, apparently to reopen the shop, shooing Farrin away.

Farrin and Graham fought the wind with every step to the Metro and shivered as they rode down the escalator. "What was that about?" Graham asked.

"He was supposed to be here two hours ago, but when I called, he acted like I'd never asked him to cover for me. He's the only employee who isn't friends with either the bride or groom."

"Where is this wedding?" Graham shouted over the roar of the train.

"Saint Genesius." Farrin hustled through the turnstile and sprinted for the train. It occurred to Graham that the way Farrin moved seemed stronger, healthier.

"Saint Genesius? Either we're not thinking of the same church, or I misheard you. I thought you said we're crashing a wedding, not a rave."

"The guests will be confused, too. Arches and stained glass windows outside, and inside, three bars and the stale odor of last night's club fog. But I've heard weddings have been held there on occasion." Farrin rubbed Graham's cheek, either to brush away lint from his scarf or perhaps for the sake of contact. Graham blushed.

"They need room for a thousand people?" Graham wondered

who could afford renting such a massive space.

"Yes, and the sound system. There'll be a reception at the Willard Hotel afterward to make up for the metal folding chairs. My sister couldn't talk my parents out of that."

Graham froze, an ache circling his heart.

"We're crashing your—" Graham noticed the passengers around them staring and lowered his voice. "You're not invited to your sister's wedding?"

Farrin took a deep breath. "Another thing my sister couldn't talk my parents out of."

"Which sister?"

"Rekha. My younger sister."

Graham knew enough about Asian traditions to understand Farrin's two older sisters must have married in the three years since he'd seen him. "Were you invited to Sonia's wedding? Or Anjani's?"

"No. They told my parents they wanted me there, but I was in hospital anyway. Sonia and her husband own the bird shop. They do a lot for me."

Graham looked away as Farrin rubbed his forehead. He searched for a new topic, something unrelated to weddings.

"Do you know what I read about your favorite song? It's really about hobos taking a ride in the boxcar of a train in California. And there's an earthquake."

"'Here Comes Your Man?' I've read that. Or it's about dropping the bomb on Hiroshima. I think it's too happy for either of those. It gives me the image of a wedding, actually."

So much for changing the subject.

"I see a sad, impoverished bride waiting in a homemade dress with her farmer parents and a preacher. They're standing by a rotting wagon that's been in the same spot for so long it's a landmark. She has a bouquet of wildflowers she picked on the way. It's drizzling. No one is talking. I think her husband-to-be is a soldier, maybe during the Civil War, and she hasn't seen him in years."

"Three years, perhaps?"

Farrin looked puzzled. Then he raised his eyebrows at Graham and smiled. "Exactly! This was the day they'd planned to marry, but they don't know if he's coming or is even alive. And then, *pow*, there he is, walking over the rise. She smiles the prettiest smile, and it's the happiest moment anyone's had ever."

"I like that," Graham said, noting that even in Farrin's fantasies, the wedding was a hetero one. The train rolled to a stop.

Graham had never seen so many suits and tuxes at Genesius. The two of them stayed on the far side of the street, giving the crowd a wide berth until they neared a service entrance. Farrin knocked twice before someone answered. The scrawny Vietnamese fellow who usually monitored the club's VIP area peeked out. "Farrin, good to see you. Will you be okay out in the cold for a bit?"

Farrin nodded.

"I'll prop this open for heat, but wait five minutes for everyone to be seated. Close the door behind you, and then take the stairs on the right. All the way up."

They huddled, Farrin checking his watch every thirty seconds, and then went to a staircase that appeared long unused. The dust was terrible, and Graham's coughing fit would have given them away if the music hadn't started at that moment. Farrin rubbed Graham's back to soothe him.

Swelling, ethereal keyboards were joined by a dreamy, angelic female voice. It seemed both triumphant and bursting with bliss.

Farrin clapped his hands. "'Fotzepolitic' by The Cocteau Twins. She did it. She took my idea."

The music sounded like something they should play when you arrived in heaven. Still Graham asked, "You suggested this instead of The Pixies?"

Farrin watched Rekha and his father walk down the enormous aisle. "This is the song I'd want for something big. Something beautiful, but grand. But when I get married in the rain next to a rotting wagon, I want 'Here Comes Your Man.'"

Graham closed his eyes and let the music fill him. The voice made him want to cry, to kiss, to grab Farrin in the tightest hug and never let go. Considering how much music affected Farrin, he had to be feeling something similar.

He opened his eyes to watch Farrin cover his mouth with his hand, perhaps to conceal a trembling lip. Then Graham looked below, noticing Rekha's white dress, confused for a moment as he'd thought South Asian brides wore red. Then he noticed Farrin's father's attire. Not a tux, but a gaudy uniform with... was that a crown?

Tracy used the word "exile." Farrin's blog is called Revelations of a Royal Mess.

"You're—you're a prince?"

Farrin continued to stare at the wedding but shook his head. "No. I mean, yes, but there hasn't been a raja in Kashmir since the 1940s. All this pomp is crazy. It's fun to say I'm royalty, but it's also silly. I'm not anyone special."

Graham squeezed Farrin's arm. "Yes, you are."

Farrin glanced quickly at Graham and then looked away. "You're right. I am. Thank you." Then his eyes lit up and he pointed. "See Rekha's bouquet?"

Graham saw what looked like a spray of paperwhite narcissus with a single blue flower poking out.

"That's her something blue?"

"A cornflower. It's my favorite. She told me she'd have one

as—I guess a silent protest."

Graham nodded. As Rekha passed the front row of guests, Graham noticed the bridesmaids. "Sonia and Anjani each have a blue flower tucked behind an ear."

Farrin's head jerked in surprise as he looked at his sisters.

Graham scanned the room. "There's a gentleman with a blue flower in his lapel in the third row. And the woman two rows in front of him appears to have a blue corsage."

"That's my mother." Farrin was now clearly overwhelmed. "This is good. Let's go."

Graham grabbed Farrin's hand. "Don't you want to stay to hear their vows?"

"I promised to see her walk down the aisle. And if she did use my music, I was wondering if it would be how I imagined."

"Was it?"

"Better." Farrin swiped at his eyes.

"I'm sorry this is upsetting you."

Farrin smiled. "I've never been happier."

Graham accompanied Farrin back to the Federal Department of Parakeets, looking for an excuse to see him again. The fact that Farrin was a prince without Graham's knowing, despite his attempts at research, felt confusing. Recalling that research triggered his guilt.

"I know I apologized before, but if the way I *checked* on things is what made you leave three years ago…"

"It wasn't. I was put in treatment by my father."

"That must have been awful."

"I didn't want to go. But it was good. The man with the flower behind my mother? That's my uncle. Most of my dad's family went into running hotels and playing polo after my great-grandfather abdicated, but my uncle became a psychiatrist. He argued with my father until he agreed to send me to England to be treated for depression instead of the religious curative clinic he'd chosen himself. I got what I needed."

"I also need to confess," Graham continued, "I'm still looking you up. I read the post on your blog a few months ago. It sounded encouraging, but I shouldn't have—"

"I was hoping you'd see it. Otherwise I wouldn't have left 'Kabul Bombs the Bass' as the pass code." Farrin shivered and blew on his hands.

The man who'd relieved Farrin earlier came bursting through the doors, spat angry words at Farrin, and took off without waiting for a response.

"What did he say?"

"Just personal barbs mixed with phobic rhetoric not worth translating."

Graham could tell Farrin was frustrated and changed the subject. "I'll let you go, but I'd like to see you again."

Farrin's lips tightened. "I've wanted very much to see you, but there are reasons why I haven't. Give me your email address and I'll explain."

Graham wasn't discouraged. Since learning he wasn't the reason for Farrin's disappearance, his mood had buoyed. "A quick kiss," he said, pressing his lips to Farrin's soft cheek. "I look forward to hearing everything."

That evening, Graham waited impatiently in his office chair for Farrin's email. He was on his third mug of hot chocolate. He'd downloaded the Cocteau Twins' song from Rekha's wedding and listened to it several times. Around eleven, he was about to give up, but finally it came.

> *My health has improved. Learning to forgive and to be thankful has changed me, and except for a bit of loneliness, I'm happy with life.*

However, there are limitations. Parakeets don't care if I have bad ADD as long as I feed them and make sure they get attention, and I'm focused enough now to use a cash register. But even end-of-day bookkeeping can be a problem. Sonia had to hire someone (the man you saw) to ensure it's done correctly, and business isn't what it needs to be.

If someday I have to obey my father's wishes and marry a woman, I hope Tracy will be able to find me a friend of hers in a similar situation. Even more, I don't want to hurt you if ultimately I have to leave. But I miss you and think of you every day.

Graham shook his head. Farrin seemed so happy, but what if the store failed and Farrin couldn't find other work? The possibility of needing help from someone who thought so little of him must feel awful. He wrote a short reply.

Handsome Prince:

You're doing so well, and maybe things could get even better. I've been looking into self-improvement myself, and what do you know? The course "Bookkeeping for Birds" was exactly my plan.

By the next day, Graham had received only one response with a smiley face, and the message, *Handsome prince, eh? Please don't spend money on something that doesn't interest you. But the idea is sweet. Thank you so much.*

Graham responded by sending a copy of his registration for a class beginning the next week.

After another four days passed, he hoped Farrin had discovered his other surprise. He was about to go to the Department of Parakeets when Farrin called.

"It's been unbelievably busy," Farrin said. "I couldn't understand why until a customer gave me a clipping from the *Washington City Paper* saying this store is the 'go-to place for feathered friends in the Capital area.' I wonder how they learned that?"

Graham could hear the amusement in Farrin's voice and said, "Those journalist types are sneaky."

"It reads here that 'employee Farrin Zafrani ensures that potential buyers are asked the right questions, so they know for certain which bird is best suited for their homes and which will be the best companions.' The article is attributed to a fellow named Graham Andrews."

"Farrin, I know you're scared things might not work out for you, but please let me be the guy you can depend on."

There was a pause. Then Farrin said, "I'd like that. I really would."

Graham felt elation pour through him, starting in his gut and flowing down to his toes and up to his broad grin.

"We close in an hour. Do you feel like helping me dance with some birds after I lock up? Then maybe dinner someplace cheap?"

"You got it, mister. Here comes your man."

STRUCK

'Nathan Burgoine

I'm going to fix your life!"

Chris balanced a dozen copies of the latest teen hardcover in his left arm. The customer who'd spoken had just walked by his boss Laurali, who was at the cash registers leafing through a magazine. Why customers avoided obviously free staff to ask questions of the employee with his hands full was one of the mysteries of working at Book It.

"Is that the title?" Chris asked.

"What?"

"I'm going to fix your life," Chris repeated. The books were getting heavier by the moment. It was probably all the angst.

"No," the customer said. "I am."

"Pardon?" Chris tried not to stare at him.

The customer was trim, blond and had eyes an impossible shade of blue—Chris could see the contacts. He was tanned and sporting a skintight blue shirt the precise shade of his contacts, as well as a deep frown.

"Oh!" the customer said. "You think I'm looking for a book!" He laughed, as if he'd just gotten the joke.

This is *a bookstore*, Chris wanted to say. Instead, aware that Laurali was now looking at him—Chris could feel her "disappointed" stare burning a hole in the back of his head—he said, "How may I help you?"

"No, no," the blond repeated, chuckling now. His teeth were so bleached they dazzled. "I'm here to help you, uh…" His eyes glanced down to Chris's name tag. "Chris."

Was he being scouted? For a brief instant, Chris allowed himself the fantasy. This blond was going to swoop in, hire him to be the manager at a beautiful gallery somewhere incredibly warm all year round—it would have to be, given the blond's tan—and…and…uh. Maybe a beach?

Oh my god. I've lost the ability even to fantasize about a better life.

"Okay," Chris said, coming back to reality. More likely the blond was about to offer him a personal connection to Jesus Christ. If Jesus Christ would take the damned teen books out of his arms, Chris would consider it.

"I'm Lightning Todd."

"Okay," Chris said, wary. Maybe this was a joke? Lightning Todd? *Oh god. He's a stripogram. I'm going to get fired.*

Lightning Todd frowned again. "Don't you know who I am?"

"Lightning Todd?" Chris said gamely. The back of his head had to be smoking by now. He could hear Laurali sighing theatrically at the cash desk.

The blond nodded. "The one and only. So, here's the thing. I've tuned in on you, which, as you know, is totally awesome."

"Totally." Chris shifted the books from his left arm to his right. Tolstoy didn't weigh this much. Shouldn't classics weigh more than teenaged hormones? "Listen, I'm really flattered, but I'm at work right now." He offered his best smile.

"What?" Lightning Todd frowned again. It didn't seem to take much to confuse him. "Oh!" His eyes widened. "Oh my god, no! I'm not hitting on you. You're *old*!"

Chris's teeth clenched. "I'm thirty-six."

"Really?" Lightning Todd peered at him. "I wouldn't have said more than thirty-two. Well done."

"Thank you." Chris felt his face reddening. "Listen, I need to get these dealt with." He lifted the hardcovers slightly. "So if there's nothing I can help you with…"

Lightning Todd shook his head. "You're not open to it right now. But listen, after the coffee issue and the zipper thing, I'll come back, and we'll chat again, okay," Lightning Todd paused and glanced again at Chris's nametag, "Chris?"

"Sure." *The coffee issue and the zipper thing?*

Lightning Todd nodded and walked past him. Chris could have sworn he heard the blond mutter "Thirty-six!" under his breath with something like disgust. When Chris got to the cash registers, Laurali was scowling at him.

"Friend of yours?" she asked. Chris reminded himself that she was only a temporary problem. Laurali was covering Tracey's maternity leave. Tracey was the greatest boss Chris had ever had. Laurali, Chris was sure, had been sent by his own personal devil to make his life as miserable as possible. She had the worst sense of "business casual" Chris had ever encountered—today her blouse was leopard print—and she wore faux glasses that didn't have a prescription because—her words—"people equate glasses with management."

"No," Chris said, putting down the books. His arms felt light and rubbery. "Customer."

"He couldn't have been a customer," Laurali said. Her voice

was singsong upbeat. That meant trouble.

"He wasn't a friend," Chris repeated. Laurali hated it when the staff had friends drop by. Unless they were hers.

"But if he was a customer, you didn't convert him from a browser to a buyer." Laurali looked over her glasses—and down her nose—at him. She held up a finger. "Remember the mantra: *Conversion is King!* You may be only an assistant manager, but if you don't model the behavior, how will the rest of the staff buy into it?"

"We're the only two people on shift." *And you've been reading that gossip magazine all morning.*

Laurali shook her head. "This is the attitude problem I was talking about at our last rap session."

"I need to put these on the display," Chris responded before he said something else that he'd regret.

Or enjoy.

He grabbed the books and turned sharply, slamming into the customer who'd appeared with ninja stealth behind him. The coffee the woman was carrying went all down Chris's front, covering his vest, shirt and half the hardcovers.

"I'm so sorry," Laurali said. She sounded positively cheerful. "He's such a klutz."

On the roof of the mall, there were manicured green spaces, plant boxes and even some trees. It was Chris's favorite place to take his break—especially now that autumn was bringing a lovely coolness to the air. It was serene. Calming. He could even see the river.

"Just four more months. I only have to make it four more months. If I killed her, I'd go to jail," he said aloud, peeling his orange. "So that's out."

"I'll pretend I didn't hear that."

Chris jumped. One of the security guards—the best security guard, in Chris's opinion—was smiling at him. He had his hands hooked into the front of his vest, which made his biceps strain the fabric of the gray shirt he wore underneath. His name was Liam. Chris had once placed an order for him for some science fiction books. Liam had a great smile that tilted a little on the left side. Also he was tall and had no wedding ring. It was enjoyable to watch him come and go through the mall. Especially go.

The uniform pants were really snug in the behind.

Chris had noticed that Liam took his breaks on the rooftop garden a few months before and had been all the more vigilant to use the green space himself since. Which had a downside, apparently.

"How long have you been standing there?" Chris asked. He felt his cheeks burning.

"Long enough to learn that you're planning to murder your boss because she's a hypocritical harpy. And passive aggressive." Liam's eyes flicked down. "What happened to your shirt?"

"I bumped into a customer and she spilled coffee all over me. You realize now that you've heard my plotting, you know too much, right?"

Liam laughed. "I'm pretty sure I could take you."

Yes, please. Chris's tongue glued itself to the top of his mouth. "Gluh."

"What?" Liam asked. He had the most expressive brown eyes. Right now they were expressing amusement. Or maybe pity.

Chris came back to earth. "Nothing, sorry. I promise not to kill anyone today."

"Or in four months?"

Chris sighed. "In four months my real boss comes back from maternity leave, and Laurali will be a bad memory."

"Can you make it four months?"

"I'll try. Murder is so messy. And you know my plans." Chris smiled. He loved Liam's slightly crooked grin.

"At least wait until I'm off today. I have an important dinner tonight."

"Sounds like fun." Chris wondered if he could sound more moronic if he really, really tried. This was the most they'd ever talked, and he could feel his IQ dropping the longer he spoke.

"We're having a big anniversary dinner. My folks are in town."

We. He must have a girlfriend. He and his girlfriend are celebrating their anniversary, and even his parents are coming. She's such a lucky woman. I hate her.

Chris nodded. "Cool." *Cool? That's all you can say?*

Liam nodded. Chris nodded back. He was pretty sure it couldn't get more awkward.

"Uh." Liam sounded apologetic. "Your fly is open."

I want to die. Chris reached down and zipped up. "Thanks." He wondered if Laurali had noticed, and if she had, how long she'd enjoyed knowing he looked foolish.

Liam nodded and then walked back to the doors. Chris rubbed his eyes. This was turning into a truly bad day. His phone chirped. He had five minutes to get back to the store before he'd be late from his break. The last thing he needed was to give Laurali any more ammunition. She'd hated him from the first day of Tracey's maternity leave.

He tossed the half-peeled orange into the garbage can beside the door. Liam had a girlfriend and they were having an anniversary. Even if it were not an unrequited crush, between the coffee issue and the zipper thing, all hope would have been lost anyway.

Something about that nibbled at the back of Chris's thoughts for the rest of his shift.

* * *

"See?"

Chris counted to five, put his smile in place and turned around. It was Lightning Todd again, though this time his contacts—and his T-shirt—were both a deep green.

"Hi," Chris said. He had a cart full of books to shelve, and Laurali had been on the warpath about their lagging conversion numbers after she'd gotten a call from the regional manager about the store's flagging sales. If Chris heard "Conversion is King!" one more time, he would vomit. Not that Laurali had been actively talking to customers herself or anything.

Lightning Todd spread his hands wide. "Well?"

"I'm sorry?" Chris frowned.

"The coffee?" Lightning Todd rubbed his left hand across his chest. Then he pointed his right index finger at his crotch, bouncing his arm up and down. "The zipper?"

Chris stared. It looked like Lightning Todd was doing some sort of erotic dance.

"Chris!" Laurali's voice was loud in the nearly empty store. "No friends. We've talked about this."

Lightning Todd turned and glared at her. "I'll just be, like, a minute. Don't freak out." Laurali's eyes bugged out behind her glasses. Lightning Todd turned back to Chris, and in a whisper that was louder than his already boisterous voice, he added, "What a colossal bitch."

That's it, Chris thought. *I'm fired.* "What do you want?"

"The coffee and the zipper. Called it, right?" The blond looked inordinately pleased with himself.

Chris blinked. He had, hadn't he? "How—" He shook his head. When had he lost control of this conversation? "Listen, I don't get the joke, but I'm at work. If I can help you find something, I will, but otherwise—"

"You don't get it." The blond shook his head. "I go where I'm needed. Ever since That Day." He said the two words with feeling. Chris had no idea what he was talking about, and it apparently showed. "Didn't you check out my website?"

"You have a website?"

Lightning Todd sighed. "Listen. Here's the sitch. I only tune in on people who need me. And you need me bad, Chris." He nodded briskly.

"I thought I was too old for you."

"What?" The blond frowned. "Oh! Ha. You're funny. But listen. Before you quit and never come back, you totally have to kiss the guy who won't wear pink."

"Kiss the... Before I quit?" Given his situation, that was rather unlikely.

"Because of the *Titanic*."

"Because of the *Titanic*." Chris leaned forward. "Are you high? Do you need me to call someone for you?"

"Chris!" Laurali called. She was using her singsong voice again.

"Ugh." Lightning Todd rolled his eyes. "She's horrible. Her vibes are, like, sticky and smell like purple. Anyway, the sixes and ones will make everything better, once you're stuck for a way to go home."

"Chris, I need you to finish the shelving." Laurali had come out from behind the counter for the first time all day. She gave Lightning Todd a tight smile and looked over the top of her glasses at him. "I'm afraid you'll have to go. It's company policy not to allow friends to interfere with our employees while they work."

"You know," Lightning Todd said, "if you got over the whole cheated with a gay guy thing your husband did, you'd be open to some bliss and stuff."

Laurali went white. "Get out."

Lightning Todd shrugged. "I'll see you Friday night at Bitter-sweets?" It took Chris a moment to realize Lightning Todd was speaking to him.

"I close the store Friday night."

"You might be free," Lightning Todd said and shook his head. He made two finger guns. "Todd has spoken. You've been struck." Then he trotted away.

Laurali stared at Chris. Her neck was turning red. "Shelve the cart," she snapped.

Chris nodded and got back to work.

"I didn't take you for the techno sort."

Chris glanced up at Liam from the bench on the rooftop garden. Liam was doing the "undercover" thing today—though it was easy enough to tell he had the vest on under his hoodie. He was wearing a pink cap, though, which surprised Chris and made him think of Lightning Todd's words. Obviously, Liam was a guy who would wear pink. No kissing him.

Also: girlfriend, he reminded himself.

"I'm not," Chris said. He held up his phone. "It's a website."

Liam sat beside him on the bench and looked at the screen. "Lightning Rod?"

"Lightning Todd," Chris said.

"Is that a stripper?"

"See!" Chris felt vindicated. "That's what I thought."

Liam's eyebrows rose. They were good eyebrows, even if he did look a little dorky in a pink ball cap.

"He's a psychic, apparently," Chris said.

Liam laughed.

Chris shrugged. "He got hit by lightning a few years back.

Ever since, he says he can…" Chris looked at the little screen. "Tune in to the vibes of the universe and help people find their bliss." Chris winced. "He used the contraction for 'they are' instead of the possessive."

"Sounds completely legit." Liam smirked.

Chris thumbed off the phone. The pounding bass stopped. For a second, he thought about telling Liam about the coffee and zipper thing, but he felt a little stupid for considering Lightning Todd's advice. Quitting because of the *Titanic?* He shook his head.

"So how was the anniversary dinner? Did she love it?"

Liam seemed surprised. "Yeah. It was nice."

Chris smiled. His phone chirped. He groaned. "That's my five-minute warning."

"Time to go back to the hypocritical harpy?"

"You have a good memory. I shouldn't have plotted murder in front of you." Chris gave Liam's shoulder a shove. Now that Liam was completely unavailable, it was much less daunting to talk to him.

Liam laughed. "I should get back to looking for shoplifters."

"And I have an entire cart of romance novels to shelve. Our lives overflow with excitement." He stood and the two walked back into the mall together.

"What else would you do?" Liam asked. "If you weren't married to romance novels."

Chris looked at him. It wasn't a question he was often asked. But it didn't need any thought. "I'd work at a museum. The National Art Gallery, if I could. I have most of an Art History degree."

"Most?"

Chris nodded. They stepped onto the escalators.

"I had to drop out third year. My father died."

Liam flinched. "I'm sorry."

"It's okay. He had a heart attack and hadn't put a will together. My parents were living check to check. My mother ended up bankrupt. I got the job at the bookstore part-time to help pay for university, but it ended up becoming a permanent gig after that, so I could help keep her afloat." He smiled. "I do like the job."

They were at the bottom of the escalator.

"Except for the harpy."

"Except." Chris nodded. He was a little surprised that Liam had asked, and more surprised that he'd answered honestly. It was easier to be candid when you weren't trying to impress someone.

"What about you?" Chris asked.

"Give up all this?" Liam raised his arms.

Chris laughed. He was running out of break time. He turned to go.

"Photographer," Liam said. "Black and white."

Chris smiled. "So we're both art lovers." Liam nodded, and Chris headed for the store. A few paces away, he turned back. "Kudos for having the guts to sport the hat, by the way."

"What?" Liam asked.

"Very Don Johnson." Chris gave Liam a thumbs-up before he turned and went back to Book It.

"The *Titanic* had to be sunk, you know."

Chris froze. He'd been walking by the transportation section with an armload of *Curious George* when a customer reached out and took his shoulder. He was an older man, with bushy gray eyebrows and a slightly manic smile.

Chris stepped back, but the man's grip stayed firm. "We have a couple of books on the *Titanic* right there." He gestured. He felt a little tremble in his stomach. *The Titanic.*

"None of them are right."

"I'm sorry?" Chris twisted a little bit, and the man finally removed his hand.

"There were too many real people on board. That's why they had to sink the *Titanic.*"

Do not engage. Be polite. Move on. "I'm afraid that's all we have. They might have more selection at one of our other locations."

"If you squint just right, you can tell who's real and who isn't." The man reeked of mouthwash. Chris felt bad for him. His clothes were a bit heavy for the season and none too clean. Maybe he was homeless. "Too many real people wanted to ride the *Titanic.* Made themselves a target. They don't want the real people to live."

"I see." Chris glanced toward the front, but Laurali was talking to Jason, the only other staff member in the store. She seemed to be giving him crap about something. Of course.

The man squinted at him. "You're real."

This wasn't comforting, given what Chris had learned about real people thus far.

"I'm afraid that's all we have," Chris repeated.

The man took both books from the shelf and started walking toward the front of the store. Chris hesitated. A moment later, it became obvious the man wasn't headed to the registers, and he caught up with him.

"Did you want me to put those at the register for you?" he asked, raising his voice a little. Laurali, however, didn't stop her ranting. Chris heard the word "conversion" and tried not to groan.

The man's eyebrows rose high on his forehead.

"You're real!" he said.

"I've heard that." Chris reached for the books. "I can put these on hold for you, if you'd like."

The man bellowed at him, an inarticulate noise that was louder than Chris would have thought his slim frame could produce. Then he threw the books on the floor and ran from the store.

"Okay," Chris said, shaken.

"What was that?" Laurali's voice was back to that grating singsong. Chris knelt and picked up the two books. One was ripped.

"He was a little confused. He was going to leave without paying, so I offered to put the books on hold, and he lost it."

"You're not supposed to confront thieves," Laurali said.

"I thought we were supposed to offer them extra help so they know they've been spotted," Jason said. Chris could have hugged him.

"Not if they're dangerous or determined. Then you're supposed to let the manager know and have security called." Laurali shook her head. "I'm disappointed, Chris. That could have been handled better."

"I tried to get your attention. You didn't look at the floor even once."

Laurali bristled. "I'll call security now and see if they can apprehend him."

"No, don't. He was just confused. I think he might have been homeless."

"Then he shouldn't be in the mall. They need to ban him." She picked up the phone. "What did he look like?"

"I don't really remember," Chris said.

Laurali put the phone down and looked at him over the top of her glasses.

* * *

"You're writing me up for insubordination." Chris tried not to grind his teeth.

Laurali shook her head sadly. "Chris, you're struggling. I'm not sure why you have such a problem with policy and professionalism..."

Count to five. Just count to five.

"...but it can't go on like this." Laurali sighed. "I know you had a different relationship with Tracey, but I expect a level of propriety."

"Propriety?"

"Yes. The way you undermined me in front of Jason, and your friend who kept making those obscene gestures... It's not okay."

One. Two. Three. Three and a half.

"We have customers who find your lifestyle upsetting."

"Lifestyle?" Chris's voice grew even.

Laurali crossed her arms. "This is what I'm talking about. You're defensive. You're aggressive. Frankly, I find you hostile."

Chris forgot to count. "I find you lazy. And you're a hypocritical, passive-aggressive bitch. You possess half the humanity found in a clogged drainpipe. With less style."

Laurali's eyes widened. Her lips narrowed. She took a breath.

"Chris," she started.

Chris held up his hand. "Don't ruin this with words. I quit."

He left her in the back room, walked to the front of the store and passed Jason at the cash desk.

"I just quit. I told her she was a bitch. Sorry about the rest of your afternoon."

"You're my hero," Jason said.

Chris kept walking. He made it all the way to the bus station before he realized that his bus pass was in his jacket, which was in the back room of Book It.

"Thought I might find you here."

Chris sat with his back against one of the trees on the rooftop garden. He frowned at Liam. "Pardon?"

Liam was doing his undercover thing again. No ball cap, though. "We got a call from your boss. She wanted to make sure you left the premises."

Chris sighed. "Fantastic. My bus pass is still in the store. I was waiting here until she left for the day, and then I was going to ask my coworker... my *former* coworker...to get it for me."

"You okay?" Liam sat down on the grass beside him.

"I really needed that job. My mother..." He sighed. "Well."

"I get it. I'm close to my parents, too, obviously." Liam gave Chris's shoulder a squeeze.

Chris wasn't so sure what was obvious about it, but it was a nice sentiment.

"I guess I should go get my bus pass and head out. I'd hoped never to see her again." Chris rubbed his eyes. "I kind of told her she was a complete bitch. And had no style."

"Harsh." Liam's lips were twitching.

"I may have also intimated she was without a soul."

"I'll walk you. That way she can't pitch a fit."

"Thanks."

They rode the escalator in silence. When he arrived at the store, Laurali held up one hand before he even crossed the threshold.

"You're not allowed in here. I've filled in the paperwork, and you'll be served with a trespass notice as soon as home office approves it."

"Super. I just need my bus pass, and then I'll happily never see you again." Chris looked for Jason and saw him at the back of the store with a customer. "If you'll get it for me, I'll leave and never look back, you miserable harpy."

Liam took his shoulder and squeezed. Chris took the hint and tried to calm down.

"I mailed your belongings already," Laurali said. Her voice was triumphant.

"Pardon?"

"As per policy, I packed up your belongings and took them to the post office. Now please escort him out of the mall." Laurali looked over her glasses at Liam.

"Do you want to go?" Liam asked. Chris took a moment to enjoy the look of frustration that crossed Laurali's face.

"Gladly," Chris said and turned around. Once Book It was out of sight, Chris sighed. "Is it okay if we swing by the lotto booth before I'm banned from the mall so I can buy bus tickets?"

"Of course. And you're not banned from the mall. She can't do that."

"You'll forgive me if I never come back."

"That'd be disappointing."

Chris glanced at him, surprised by the comment. It was sweet. Which was probably why his girlfriend loved him so much. Liam looked slightly uncomfortable, and Chris forced himself to smile. No point in being morose. They walked to the lotto booth and got in line.

Liam chuckled.

Chris glanced at him. "What?"

"Miserable harpy." Liam's lips twitched. "Sorry. I know it's not funny."

"I feel kind of bad about it."

Liam look surprised.

"It's an unfair comparison. Harpies aren't so bad."

Liam laughed. Chris liked his laugh. Ahead of them, a woman was apparently buying years' worth of lottery tickets. The poor clerk had pulled out all three trays from the plastic cover that ran across the countertop. Chris took a deep breath. He was amazed at how much better he felt, even if he had just quit his job. Book It had been awful since the day Tracey left, but he'd forced himself not to think about it. Because of his mother.

That was going to depress him again, so he decided to change the subject. He smiled at Liam. "No cap today?"

Liam scowled. "No. Thanks for giving me the heads-up."

The woman in front of them stepped aside, a few dozen pieces of paper in hand, and Chris stepped up. The clerk said, "I just need to put these away."

Chris nodded. "Take your time." The clerk gave Chris a grateful smile. Chris turned back to Liam. "What do you mean? What heads-up?"

Liam shook his head. "The security guys were playing a trick on me."

"I don't get it."

"What can I help you with?" the clerk asked.

"I need a sheet of bus tickets, please."

"Seven-eighty," the clerk said and turned to open a drawer.

Chris dug into his pockets and then closed his eyes. "Crap. My wallet was in my coat. Which Laurali just mailed to me." He fished through his pockets and came up with a five-dollar bill and a bunch of coins. He put them on the counter and started sorting them. "Sorry," he said. "Go on."

"They know I'm colorblind. The pink cap was their idea of a joke. Make the gay guy wear pink. I thought it was gray."

"Oh," Chris said. He pushed a stack of dimes and two quarters to the side. That was six dollars. Then he stopped. "Wait. What?"

Liam shrugged. "They're kind of jerks. Not all of them, but..." He shrugged.

"Your anniversary was with your boyfriend, not your girlfriend," Chris said.

"I don't have a boyfriend. Why would I flirt with you if I had a boyfriend?"

"You've been flirting with me?"

Liam was turning red. "Well...yeah."

"But you had an anniversary dinner."

"My parents' anniversary. I told you that."

"No, you didn't."

"Sure I did..." He paused. "Didn't I?"

"No."

"But you asked how my mother liked it," Liam said.

"No, I asked how your girlfriend liked it."

"I don't have a girlfriend."

"Yeah, I got that part now."

Someone's throat cleared. Chris turned. A woman was standing behind him. As were three people behind her. All of them were watching.

"Go ahead," Chris said and stepped aside. The clerk moved to help her. Chris took Liam's arm. It felt strong. His hand shook.

"You've been flirting with me?"

"You started it," Liam said. "Up in the garden."

"Because I thought you were straight."

"You flirt with straight guys?" Liam raised an eyebrow.

"No." Chris laughed. "I just... I'd relaxed... I figured you weren't available, and that... Wow. Thank god for pink hats."

"I don't wear pink," Liam said.

"Lightning Todd," Chris said.

"The psychic stripper?"

"I have to kiss you before I go," Chris said. The moment the words were out of his mouth, he wanted to take them back. Liam was grinning and Chris felt his skin burning. Had he really just said that?

"I can live with that," Liam said.

"Don't mind us," one of the customers said behind them. Chris closed his eyes, mortified, but a second later, he felt Liam's fingers on his chin. He opened his eyes and saw Liam leaning forward. They kissed. Liam's chin was a little rough with stubble, and Chris didn't mind a bit.

"Suddenly I'm not having a bad day at all," Chris said.

The clerk and the two remaining customers gave them a small round of applause. Liam looked past him and blushed.

"You need your tickets?" the clerk asked.

"Yeah," Chris said. He turned back to the counter and— fingertips shaking a little—resumed counting his coins.

"Do you have enough?" Liam asked. He put his hand back on Chris's shoulder. It felt good there.

"I think so." Chris moved aside a coin and looked through the clear plastic at the lottery ticket beneath where he'd been counting.

The numbers caught his eye: 1. 6. 11. 16. 61. 66.

"Ones and sixes," he said. It was a scratch-and-win: one of those tickets with a grand payout of cash every week for life. "Ones and sixes when I'm stuck for a way home."

"What?" Liam asked.

"Can I get that ticket, too?" Chris said, pointing. The clerk nodded and pulled out the tray.

"That'll be twelve-eighty."

Chris looked at his pile of change, then at Liam. "If I told you I had a good feeling about this, would you go halfsies with me?"

Liam smiled and pulled out his wallet.

At the mall exit, they kissed again. Chris grinned. "Friday night, what are you doing?"

"I work here until five, but after that, I'm all yours," Liam said.

"Ever been to Bittersweets?"

"The coffee place? Yeah."

"It's a date," Chris said. "Six?"

"You got it." Liam sighed and rubbed his chin. "It really sucks I won't see you until Friday night."

"Two days is a long time to wait," Chris agreed. "How about tonight I make you dinner. I suddenly have free time on my hands."

Liam winced. "I'm sorry about your job. Are you okay?"

Chris nodded. "I feel good about it. Let me give you my number. I live near Bronson and Sommerset."

They exchanged numbers, tapping them into their phones. Then Liam rolled back on his heels. "I should go back."

"I know."

"You gonna scratch that on the bus?" Liam asked.

Chris was clutching the lottery ticket. He shook his head. "Nope. Half is yours, remember? How about I keep it for dessert?"

Liam laughed. "Sure thing. I'll see you later."

Chris got on the bus and looked out the window as the mall disappeared behind him. He found himself smiling. When someone flounced into the seat beside him, he glanced over.

"Can I call it or what?"

Lightning Todd's shirt—and eyes—were a dark brown today.

"You can call it." Chris smiled. He looked down at the lottery ticket in his hand. *I hope.* "Sixes and ones."

Lightning Todd saw the ticket and grinned. "Awesome. Can I get a testimonial for my website?"

"Only if you let me fix the typos."

"What? Oh. Sure." He wrinkled his nose. "I never take the bus. Does it always smell like this?"

Chris grinned. "Quite often."

"Gross."

They rode in silence for a while.

"What was it like?" Chris asked. "Getting hit by lightning, I mean."

Lightning Todd looked at him. "Did you kiss the guy before you left the mall?"

"Yeah. I did."

The blond grinned and aimed a finger gun at him.

"Ah," Chris said.

"Okay, I can't take it. It totally smells purple in here. I'm gone." Lightning Todd got up and pulled the string. He paused, holding the bar while the bus slowed down. "I'll see you Friday," he said. "For the testimonial."

"Bittersweets," Chris agreed.

Lightning Todd smiled. "Awesome. You're gonna love your new place."

Chris blinked. "My new place?"

The blond was already moving down the steps, the door opening in front of him. "Together. With the guy who hates pink."

Then he was gone. The bus pulled away, and Chris watched Lightning Todd stop to say something to a young couple with a stroller. Chris couldn't see how they reacted.

Good luck. Chris aimed a finger gun out the window and fired at them. Then he looked at the ticket and wondered how soon he could register for classes at the university.

TOUCH ME IN
THE MORNING

Greg Herren

I woke up alone.

It wasn't the first time. It likely wouldn't be the last.

I could count on one hand the number of times a guy had spent the night with me. *Genus gay pickup* always seemed to slip out in the middle of the night, desperate to avoid that awkward conversation in the morning and the exchange of phone numbers that would never be dialed.

Against all odds, I'd hoped this time would be different.

I lay in my empty bed, eyes closed, with daylight bleeding through the blinds. I chided myself for having hoped, for even taking a moment to wonder if maybe he hadn't left.

When will you learn? Life isn't a Disney movie. Your prince may not come. Stop being such a romantic.

Was it so sentimental or too much to ask to wake up with his body spooned against mine?

It was time to face reality. I sat up and lit a cigarette. My stomach lurched against the combination of the taste of the smoke, the fur that had grown on my teeth, my swollen tongue and the aftermath of too much alcohol and tobacco from the night before.

God, I'd been drunk.

Maybe that was the best way to play it with Dennis later. Too much alcohol, too many joints, plus the depression of being dumped for the umpteenth time this year—wouldn't that justify almost anything?

I looked at the clock. It was 10:30. I closed my eyes and thought. Dennis taught an early morning aerobics class on Mondays, and then he trained clients until about eleven. He'd be free after that until late afternoon. He usually stopped by my place for a while and then went home to take a nap before his next round of classes and clients.

Of course that was why he'd left so early. He had to go to work, and I'd been sleeping the sleep of the damned, the drunk and the over-indulged. Maybe he'd tried to wake me to say good-bye, but I was too unconscious to hear him.

There might even be a note in the kitchen.

I stood, stubbed out my cigarette and stumbled to the bathroom. I looked in the mirror as I ran hot water. What I saw was worse than I'd imagined. My hair was standing up at even more bizarre angles than usual. I needed to shave. My eyes were bloodshot, and the bags under them wouldn't fit into the overhead bin on a 747. Brushing my teeth caused another wave of nausea, but I closed my eyes and focused on my breathing until it passed. I rinsed my mouth and cupped my hand for water to wash down a couple of aspirin.

Feeling somewhat better, I staggered to the kitchen.

There wasn't a note on the counter or stuck to the refrigerator.

Not a good sign.

I dug out a loaf of bread and fumbled with the twist-tie.

But maybe he was in a rush this morning.

I ate two pieces of bread to soak up whatever alcohol was still in my stomach. Dennis always said that was the best hangover cure if having a Bloody Mary or a screwdriver wasn't a possibility. I was pretty sure I couldn't tolerate even the *smell* of vodka at that moment.

Half of a joint was perched on the lip of the ashtray in the kitchen, and I lit it once I got the coffeemaker set. I took two brief hits before crushing it out with my fingers.

No need to get stoned. Just a little to take the edge off.

My stomach seemed to accept the offering of bread, and I returned to the bathroom and turned on the shower. I climbed in and let the hot water wash the smell of cigarettes and dried sweat from my body. When I'd rubbed my skin with soap and a cloth until it was red, I turned off the water. I toweled myself dry, feeling about a thousand percent better.

After I stepped into a pair of boxer briefs, I took a deep breath. When I looked in the mirror, I saw a human instead of the Creature from the Hangover Lagoon. I flexed my muscles and smiled. It still amazed me how much my body had changed in just a few months. I owed that to Dennis.

I could mentally hear him disagree: *You did the work, darlin'.*

I'd been infatuated with Dennis from the first time I saw him. His sexy smile. The way he was always so upbeat. It wasn't unusual that he always took the time to encourage his clients, but as we got to know each other, he was just as generous toward me: a dorky, newly out, twenty-five-year-old with zero self-confidence.

I was dazzled that the hot man in the red-and-black-striped

Lycra shorts and soaked white tank top would take the time to talk to me, to listen as I stared at the mirror and outlined my flaws. My underdeveloped pecs. My nonexistent abs.

Dennis would insist, *A good gym routine and a proper diet will take care of that!*

He'd become my go-to person when it came to taking care of my body, and not only at the gym. Wherever we went, he'd point to hot guys and break down everything about them that was perfect, saying I could achieve that if I wanted. He'd scold me if I ate anything unhealthy or that wasn't on my diet; he knew the person I wanted to be and was determined to help me achieve it.

What he didn't know was the person I'd started wanting *him* to be. At first, I only fantasized about him while masturbating. I replayed snapshots I'd taken in my mind of him naked in the steam room at the gym or changing his clothes in front of me.

But as our friendship developed, I realized my attraction to him wasn't only physical. If I could see that what we had was special, that our bond had become deeper than what most friends shared, why couldn't Dennis? Even other people seemed to see it. People always thought we were a couple.

When someone asked, he always said, "Oh, no, no! We're just friends."

I always smiled, thrilled that anyone could think Dennis was my boyfriend. But it hurt a little how quickly he dismissed the possibility. It wasn't so much the words as the way he said it, as though it was absurd that he could be interested in someone like me.

But how many times had he said to me that he longed for a boyfriend, someone to share his life with, to come home to every day? Every time, I'd replied in a voice calmer than I felt that of course it would happen. But I always wondered why he never saw that I loved him and could make him happy. We both wanted the same thing. Why couldn't he see how perfect we were for each other?

The coffee was ready, so I poured myself a cup. It was almost eleven. Dennis would be coming over soon, and I needed to decide how to play this. The easiest course was to pretend I didn't remember anything from last night—that I'd been so fucked up I'd destroyed all the brain cells holding the memories.

I finished my first cup of coffee and poured another as I pieced together everything that had happened the night before. I'd been brooding about my last breakup while I gulped down shots and beer, smoked joints and tried to blot out my misery.

But no matter how much alcohol I poured down my throat, no matter how much sweet marijuana smoke I inhaled, my depression only worsened. It was around two-thirty in the morning when that damned song on the loudspeakers reminded me of my last failed prince. I started crying in the middle of the dance floor at Oz, making a total idiot of myself.

I cringed. How many people had seen that?

Dennis certainly had, leaving the hot muscle boy from Dallas he'd been dancing with. He came over and threw his arms around me, saying, "We need to get you home, darlin'." I'd nodded and followed him through the crowd until we were on Bourbon Street, where he dropped his arm around my shoulders to help me walk, cooing to me the whole time.

"There, there, darlin'. It's gonna be all right. You just listen to Auntie Dennis. Everything will be all right."

I barely remembered anything about the walk home except for the comfort of his arm around my shoulder, the way his bare chest felt against my side.

And wanting him.

When we were back at my apartment, in the bedroom, he took off my shoes. I sat on the bed, looking at his beautiful body, his torso glistening with sweat from dancing.

"I love you, Dennis," I said, as he removed my socks.

"I love you, too, honey." I knew he didn't mean it the same way I did. He loved me as his friend, as his sister, not the way I wanted him to. As I'd sat on the bed, hurting and drunk, wishing he could love me, knowing that if he could I'd stop wasting my time on the men who wouldn't, I started crying again.

He'd looked at me in alarm. "Honey, don't cry. How many times do I have to tell you to stop falling in love with these guys? Sex isn't love. The sooner you understand that, it'll be so much easier on you. He's not worth it." He reached over and wiped away my tears. His brown eyes were compassionate, full of love and concern for me, and my heart ached. "You'll find the right guy, baby. You have so much to offer, and these guys—" He shook his head. "They think you're hot enough to fuck, okay? Maybe if they stuck around, they'd realize you're the real deal. You're a prize worth keeping. But they don't. It's not because of you. It's their own issues. You understand me? It isn't you."

He pulled me into a hug. I sobbed into his neck, smelling the faint scent of CK One, feeling the smoothness and warmth of his skin against my cheek. I could feel his heartbeat pulsing through his jugular vein.

I started kissing his neck; gentle little kisses, more than I'd ever dared before, something I wouldn't have done if I hadn't been drunk.

He stiffened at first and, after a moment, as though a decision had been made, he relaxed into me. I pulled him backward onto the bed and began kissing his neck in earnest because my fantasy was happening. The two of us were in my bed, and he was responding, moaning and starting to tremble. Maybe now he'd finally realize that the reason none of the other guys worked out for either of us was because I was the right one for him, the one willing to spend the rest of my life making him feel special.

Then we were both naked, and he was kissing me, our tongues testing and examining each other's mouths, our hands running up and down each other's bodies.

Just before I came, when the pleasure was almost more than I could bear, I opened my eyes and was surprised to see tears streaming down his cheeks. He made no sound, and I closed my eyes and felt my own tears coming as I launched into the shudders of my orgasm. I cried because this was what I'd always wanted. This was the reason nothing else was ever quite right. It was love that made the difference, that made it right.

Everything is going to be all right.

That had been my last thought before I fell asleep cuddled against him, his arms around me.

Only to wake up later to find him gone without a trace: no note, no nothing, like he'd never been there.

I poured myself another cup of coffee and heard his voice in my head again, saying as he had so many times before, "Your friends are your family when you're gay. You don't fuck your friends, and you don't fuck over your friends."

You don't fuck your friends.

This couldn't be the end of things. I'd go out to the verandah and sit in my deck chair, the way I did every Monday morning with my coffee, to wait for him. He'd bound into the court-yard like always, carrying a copy of the newspaper, his gym bag slung over his shoulder. He'd see me and tromp up the steps to have coffee with me, that big smile on his face, the one that lit up a room.

My stomach lurched when I heard his knock. I put down my

coffee cup, took a deep breath and walked to the door.

He looked terrible, as if he hadn't slept in a week. He held a greasy white Café du Monde bag in his left hand. His gym bag drooped over his right shoulder. His face looked haggard. Streams of sweat ran from under the purple and gold LSU baseball cap he wore backward. He had on a pair of black sweatpants and a red, sleeved T-shirt, two things he always said it was too hot to wear.

He made no move to hug or kiss me. He held up the bag.

"I stopped at Café du Monde and got beignets." His feeble smile faded almost immediately.

"I made coffee." I turned and walked into the kitchen, calling back over my shoulder for him to have a seat in the living room, that I'd bring him a cup. I wanted a moment alone in the kitchen.

My hands shook when I finally poured his coffee into the mug I always used for him, the one that said, IT'S NOT THE HEAT IT'S THE STUPIDITY. I added artificial sweetener and French vanilla creamer. While I stirred it, then refilled my own cup, I took several deep breaths. I took a swallow of coffee then steeled myself to carry both cups into the living room.

Another bad sign: Dennis sat in the recliner rather than on the couch.

He doesn't want to sit next to me. He's covered up his body with sleeves and pants. No kiss. No hug. No morning paper. No sense in giving me the wrong idea.

I took a beignet from the bag and sat on the couch.

"I can't remember the last time I had a beignet. Thanks." I smiled at him as I took a bite. It tasted like sweet sawdust; I had to force myself to chew it.

Beignets. Comfort food. Usually we both watched our diets like fat gram storm troopers.

Was this pity? *I'll bring the fat boy a sugary fried treat to make him feel better.*

But I wasn't fat anymore. That wasn't me anymore.

Are you two a couple?

No, no, no! We're just friends!

Did they feel pity for me whenever he said that? The dumpy guy following the beautiful muscle boy, lapping at crumbs like a love-starved puppy?

I took another sip of coffee.

"Is everything okay, Dennis?" I was amazed at how normal I sounded. I watched his face.

He cleared his throat. He hadn't touched either the coffee or his beignet. His face reddened.

"Last night—"

I crossed my legs and lit a cigarette when he broke off. "Yes?"

"You know I love you. I think of you like my little brother." He avoided my eyes, looking around the room, and again shifted in the chair. "The last thing I would ever want is to hurt you. You have to know that."

"I do."

"I was in a really awkward situation." He finally took a drink of his coffee. "I mean, you were so upset and depressed. I could hardly say no. It was killing me to see you so down on yourself. And for no reason. Like Blaine Tujague is worth that much suffering? But you're still so fragile about everything. I didn't want to make you feel worse." The words poured from him in an almost staccato rhythm. "My number one rule is you don't fuck your friends. It changes everything. Nothing can ever be the same. But I'd had a lot to smoke and drink myself."

Because you had to be fucked up to have sex with me?

"So I let it happen, and I'm sorry. I don't want things to be different. You're the best friend I've ever had."

He finally wound down and looked at his hands.

I forced a smile. My voice sounded hollow as I said, "I'm well aware that you don't think I'm good enough for you."

"I didn't say that." He still wouldn't look at me. His voice was a choked whisper. "I would never say that."

"You don't have to." I took a long drag off my cigarette. "Don't worry. You didn't lead me on. I know last night was nothing more than a pity fuck."

"I didn't say that either." He finally looked at me with a stricken expression.

"No. What you said was sex isn't love."

Are you a couple?

No, no, no! Of course not!

"Oh, god, I'm so sorry," he said. His eyes filled with tears, and his face twisted.

"We both made a mistake. It'll never happen again. Let's just forget about it."

I wished he'd leave.

He wiped at his eyes. "This isn't going the way I intended."

I shrugged. "I don't know—"

"I do love you."

"I know. Like a brother." I drained my cup. "I need more coffee."

I walked into the kitchen and gave the coffee pot a blank stare. I heard Dennis come up behind me. He slid his arms around my waist and put his head on my shoulder.

"Do you hate me?" he asked, barely audible.

I turned around and leaned against the counter. My heart melted at the sight of him the way it always did.

"I could never hate you. I loved you practically from the first time I saw you."

"I love you, too. And not like a brother. But you know every boyfriend I've ever had has left me. Or ended up hating me."

"That's not true," I replied automatically.

"I don't want that to happen to us. I don't want you to stop talking to me. To not be part of my life."

He kissed me, a tender little kiss. I put my arms around him and kissed him back. He tasted of coffee and Gatorade. He smelled of sweat and musk.

And he sounded like love when he said, "I'm willing to give this a try if you are."

My prince had come. I took him by the hand and led him to the bedroom.

FOUNDATIONS

Timothy Forry

*T*he hurricane is expected to pass over New England late
Saturday evening into Sunday morning...

I wanted to turn off the radio, to get some work done, but
I was too anxious. It was Friday evening, and I'd been sitting
in front of a partially blank canvas for the better part of three
hours, completely stalled. One minute I was zoned out; the next,
brought back to reality whenever the newscaster reported a new
development. My assistant caught me during one of my faraway
moments.

"You know you want to call him. I think you should."

I swiveled on my stool and looked up at Suzanne, who now
donned a long, bright-yellow rain slicker, the hood pulled over
her red hair. Her cat-eye glasses protruded beyond the frame
of the hood around her face. She looked like a librarian moon-
lighting as a lobsterwoman. I stifled a laugh.

"What?"

"Nothing," I began. "It's just that you look like..." I trailed off, stopped dead by her questioningly raised eyebrow. "I mean, it's not even raining yet."

She didn't react.

"Never mind. I'll call him. I promise."

"Good. I'm heading out. I emailed the preliminary mural sketches to the Arts Council and generated a schedule that will allow us to complete the project before the bicentennial celebration. Anything else you need?"

"No. Thank you. I'll see you on Monday morning, unless the hurricane messes things up."

"Okay, then." She was halfway out the door when she added. "Be safe, David."

When I heard the door close, I walked to the small kitchen, poured myself a cup of coffee and stared at my phone. Disconnecting it from the charger, I walked back to my stool and plopped down, placing the coffee cup on my work cart amid paintbrushes and the disarray of paint tubes.

I had no messages or texts. I could assume that everything at home was fine. Claude and Riley could manage without me. I sighed, knowing Suzanne was right. I did want to call. I touched the screen to call *Home*.

Claude picked up on the third ring. "Hello?"

When I heard his voice, my stomach tensed. I still wasn't over what he'd done; in fact, I wasn't sure I'd ever forgive him.

"It's David," I said, even more coldly than intended.

"Hi," he said quietly. Tentatively.

"How's Riley? Have the wind and rain started?"

"Riley's fine, I guess. Maybe a little anxious. Whining for no apparent reason, checking the front door more than usual. The wind's just started to pick up, and the sky's getting darker. According to the weathermen, the storm should lose a lot of power before it gets to New England."

"Okay, I just wanted to make sure..." *You're okay,* I wanted to finish, but didn't.

"Are you coming home for the weekend?"

I could hear hopefulness in his voice.

"No. I'm working through the weekend. I'm a little behind schedule."

A lie.

"We miss you."

"Yeah."

I hung up the phone. I was so torn. Hurt.

Claude and I moved to a small Vermont town with our golden retriever Riley almost four years before. We'd left New York City one autumn weekend for an impromptu foliage tour through northern Massachusetts. A wrong turn off of Route 2 led us up a winding road through the mountains, offering us grand vistas of rolling hills on fire with the blazing oranges, yellows and reds of autumn. Claude's camera worked overtime as I drove.

That fateful wrong turn led us into Vermont, where we discovered Wildmont, a quaint town on the banks of the Deerfield River. It was far removed from the frenetic energy we encountered on a daily basis in the city, even though the town was bustling with leaf-peeping tourists in the shops, galleries and restaurants. We drove through the town, which had only one traffic light.

Determined to get Claude the best possible views and photographs of the foliage, I searched side streets for any road that might lead us into the mountains that rose above Wildmont. Looking to my left, up the side of a gentle slope, I spotted Bartlet Mountain Road. It was unpaved and ragged looking, lined on either side by a dense, deciduous forest. I took the turn.

The road led sharply up the incline at first, and then leveled off, cutting across the mountain. We passed over a short, narrow bridge above a brook that tumbled over rocks as it fell down the fall line of the mountain. With the windows down, it seemed to sing to us. The air was crisp and fragrant, clean and rejuvenating. Shortly beyond the bridge, the road curved and rose again through a sparser forest, taking us to a plateau before climbing beyond. But the sight that met my eyes stopped me from driving on.

Claude lowered the camera and turned to look at me. I could tell by his expression that he shared my feelings.

We'd happened upon an old white house situated on the plateau, a simple saltbox with a stone foundation. The clearing in front of the house allowed a panoramic view of the valley. Just behind the house, the brook we'd crossed meandered across the yard before continuing its lively course downhill.

"It's for sale," Claude said, pointing toward a sign next to the mailbox at the driveway entrance.

I'd never seen such desperate longing in Claude's deep blue eyes. He clenched my hand, and I knew what we had to do.

Our call to the real estate agent was the most impetuous thing we'd ever done. After a two-minute tour, we made an offer on the house.

I pushed thoughts of home and Claude from my mind long enough to finish the left-hand side of the mural template that represented the settling of West Coxsie, New York. I was pleased with it, thus far. I cleaned my brushes in the kitchen sink and looked at the clock. It was later than I'd thought.

My email alert chimed. I walked back to my work cart and looked at the screen on my phone. My friend Alex had left New York City shortly after Bloomberg issued the evacuation order.

His email reassured me that he'd reached his family's house in Pennsylvania.

I wondered if I should tell Claude to drive up to West Coxsie with Riley, just to be safe.

I put the phone back on the work cart and shut off my studio lights. We'd had some rough storms in Vermont and everything had been fine. I was sure this would be no exception.

At first, the transition from New York to Vermont had been smoother than we could have hoped. A few years earlier, Claude and I had started a small apparel company in the city. Claude had wild ideas about handbag and backpack design, and I had the skills to execute his ideas. Over the years, we'd grown the business with minor success. Not long before our trip to Vermont, a larger apparel company had made a buyout offer. We'd refused, but the house in Wildmont provided the catalyst we needed to change our minds and accept.

Both Claude and I had needed a change. He'd felt his creativity was being stifled in the business, and I'd always wanted to pursue my passion for large-scale mural painting. The sale of the business would allow us to live comfortably, albeit frugally, for a few years as we established our new careers.

I'd been fortunate to get my first commission for a mural in a neighboring town and since then, I'd had steady work. The only problem was that I was often away from home, sometimes more than a month at a time, leaving Claude alone to look after the house and Riley.

Claude's experience was different. He'd always loved photography, and he was well trained. His eye for detail and composition, unlike any photographer with whom I was familiar, was one of the things that attracted me to him when I first met him at a group show in the city, just after he'd graduated from

Cooper Union. I was on the panel of judges.

Fortunately I'd seen his artwork before meeting him; otherwise, I might have been swayed by his good looks. He was eight years my junior, but I knew from the moment I saw him that he was an old soul. Even then, he always wore a gray tweed flat cap. His reddish brown hair poked out around the edges, as if refusing to be tamed. He wore rough-hewn shirts and either wool pants or vintage jeans. I jokingly called him my Okie.

Claude exhibited his photography in a number of galleries in Vermont, but he soon found that tourists wanted straightforward landscapes and images of foliage, as opposed to Claude's more artistic approach. He also found that it was difficult to sell to the locals and not just because of economics; they were resistant to outsiders. One of the gallery owners remarked, "They need time. It will be at least ten years before you're considered a local artist."

I worked through Saturday until I was nearly halfway done with the template. I'd finished the settlement design and made my way to the industrial boom of the early part of the twentieth century when West Coxsie was at its most vital. The mural was meant to inspire residents who'd endured a long local depression but through their own efforts were beginning to experience growth and revitalization.

Looking outside my rented studio's tall windows, I could see the sky becoming darker. I was about sixty miles northwest of Wildmont in upstate New York. I'd purposely kept the radio off and my phone silent so I could work without distractions. I checked to see if there was word from Claude and found an email.

David,

Knowing you, you've shut off the outside world so you can work, so I thought I'd give you an update. The hurricane made landfall in North Carolina and is heading toward NYC. The storm was downgraded, but it looks like it will move more northerly and not hit the coast as hard as they thought. Riley and I are bracing for wind and rain. We'll be fine, but we'd be a lot better if you were here. I understand if you're not ready yet. Or if you never will be. I'm sorry I messed everything up. I know there's no excuse, but I was so lonely and felt like a failure. I wasn't thinking clearly. Please just know that I love you. I wish I could take it all back.

Claude.

I knew he was sorry. I did. Part of me even understood why he'd cheated.

I'd been in Oregon for over a month after being home previously for only a little over a week. I'd even canceled a vacation that Claude and I had planned just so I could take the job, a mural that would cover an entire block in downtown Portland. The project was tremendous and exhausting. My team and I worked fourteen-hour days, rain or shine. My communication with Claude had been sparse. I think I'd called him twice in the span of six weeks while he was left alone on the side of a mountain.

I'd even known that his most recent showing had produced meager results and that a meeting with his gallery in the city hadn't gone well. *You've lost your edge,* the gallery owner told him.

When I'd finally returned home, I found Claude on the couch in our living room, drowning in a mound of wool blankets, haphazardly splayed magazines, and many empty beer bottles. Though only one dim light was on in the house, it wasn't hard to see that something was wrong.

"You're home," he slurred.

"What's going on?"

"I have to tell you something."

I didn't say anything and let my bags drop by my feet. Somehow I knew what he was going to say.

"I slept with someone in the city."

And there it was. As direct and tactless as he sometimes was, that was his worst delivery on record.

Over the months since his confession, my anger had mostly given way to occasional bright, throbbing jabs of fury mixed with doubt and dull depression.

I needed to get out of the studio. I wasn't consciously aware of my intentions as I drove to Mirrors, a small bar known by locals to cater to a more "colorful" crowd. The bar, a converted ranch-style house, was relatively empty for a Saturday night. It was easy to see where the name came from: the bar top was a mirror, and the back and far walls around the dance floor were floor-to-ceiling mirrors, as were all the support beams down the middle of the structure. Its tackiness seemed fitting for how displaced I felt.

I sat at the bar with an empty stool on either side of me. The bartender, an attractive, middle-aged man with a moustache, approached me as soon as I was settled.

"What's your pleasure?" he asked.

"Scotch, no ice."

I needed something strong and hard-hitting.

Drink in hand, I swung around and looked toward the dance floor, which was empty. The five high-top tables surrounding it, however, were not. I saw a cross-section of local life: a redneck couple directly across from me; next to them a well-dressed, affluent-appearing couple who were probably out "trying something different"; and against the farthest wall, slightly in the shadows, a young gay couple, probably newly in love, who weren't shy about their affection for each other.

It didn't take long for me to finish my first scotch. Without my asking, a second appeared in my hand. I turned and looked at the bartender, who was smiling, his light brown eyes sparkling.

"That one's on me. Slow tonight; we'll be closing early." He gave me a wink as he backed away.

I'd forgotten what it was like to be flirted with. I felt my face flush and threw him a half-smile.

He came from behind the bar to make his rounds, collecting the other patrons' tabs. The jukebox was suddenly silent, and the sounds of the couples gathering their belongings echoed unnervingly through the air.

I didn't move from my stool. I wasn't sure what I was doing, but I felt a twist in my gut that I hadn't felt in a long time. Was it excitement? Expectation?

Yes.

Underlying those positive, tingling emotions, a darker undercurrent crept up the back of my neck.

The light over the pool table flicked off, then the oscillating lights over the dance floor, and finally the rest of the overhead lights until it was dark save for the neon in the windows and the exit sign above the door.

The bartender appeared in front of me. He inched forward until his thighs touched the insides of my knees. He put a hand on my shoulder and looked down at me.

"My name's Derek. Let's get out of here."

* * *

I woke to the sound of rain pounding on the roof and windows of the studio. The clock on my phone displayed 10:30 a.m. The light was dull. Unaccustomed to drinking more than a glass of wine with dinner, I felt shaky from the effects of those two hefty doses of scotch. I pushed the blankets aside and went to the coffeemaker.

While the coffee brewed, I checked the news on my phone. New York City was in the eye of the hurricane. From the reports, it didn't sound nearly as bad as originally anticipated. There was some flooding in lower Manhattan, but nothing catastrophic.

Other areas along the coast hadn't been as lucky. I felt blessed to be far removed but heartsick for those whose homes were flooded or who'd lost loved ones.

Claude.

I needed to call him, but I was still struggling with the previous night's events. I was so easily seduced by the possibility of Derek. Yes, he was attractive and smooth. I thought about his warm hand on my arm, how aroused I'd been when he eased in between my legs at the bar. Had I been single, the decision would have been easy, my capitulation definite. But if I'd given in to that voice in the back of my mind that chanted, *Revenge, revenge, revenge*, its wicked counterpart would have been close behind and unbearable: *guilt.*

I was coming to realize—and couldn't believe it was something I'd taken for granted for fourteen years—how much Claude meant to me. He wasn't the only one who'd made mistakes. Change needed to happen, starting now.

I allowed myself a cup of coffee before dialing. Four rings, and then: *You've reached Claude. I might not have cell reception now, but leave a message and I'll call you back.*

"It's me. Call when you get this. We need to talk."

I turned on the radio and listened as I readied the studio for Suzanne and me to resume work on Monday. As I cleaned, the news became worse for New England. My heart sank as I heard damage reports throughout Connecticut and northern Massachusetts. High winds and torrential downpours were hitting Southern Vermont.

I tried Claude again. When he still didn't pick up, I called our neighbor, Martha, who lived in a cabin higher up on the mountain. She didn't answer, but as I was leaving a message, a call came through.

"Hello?"

"David? It's Martha."

"I've been trying to reach Claude. He hasn't returned my calls."

"I'll drive down and check the house then call you back."

I paced the studio for twenty minutes, waiting for Martha's call. The street outside my studio quickly resembled a river. Wind threw the rain against the window—harder, it seemed, as every minute passed.

Claude almost always picked up his phone. Even when he didn't, he returned calls quickly.

I didn't let the first ring finish before answering. "Martha?"

"I can't get to your house because of flooding."

"Jesus. I'm on my way."

"Stay where you are. Roads and bridges are washed out all over the place."

Maybe it was rude, but I hung up. I'd apologize later. I grabbed my coat and keys and dashed out of the studio, not bothering to lock the door behind me.

I could barely see as I drove south out of town. The road followed a stream that had risen so high it submerged the cornfield on the opposite side halfway up the stalks. There were no

major highways between West Coxsie and Wildmont, only state
roads and a scant network of back roads through the mountains. The rain kept pounding as the sun went down. I slowed
to a crawl, driving twenty miles an hour. At that rate, an hour
and a half drive would take four hours.

Late in the night, I neared the Vermont border and my heart
sank. Flashing police lights and barricades blocked my way. A
desperate discussion with a police officer yielded no favorable
result. A section of the main road was underwater and impassable. I heeded his suggestion to retreat to a motel I'd passed five
miles before.

After checking in, I lay in bed, my mind racing. I didn't sleep.
I listened to the storm. At least its monstrous roar had dimin-
ished. I propped myself up and searched maps on my phone for
any possible detours. I found one alternate route that would
circumvent the washed-out section of the main road, but it was
an unnamed passage through the mountains. If the main road
was still impassable in the morning, I'd have to risk it.

As the sky began to lighten over the hills, I left the motel.
The police barricade was gone. I turned on the radio and drove
cautiously. Fallen trees lined the road, the ground so wet their
roots could no longer support them. I dodged fallen rocks and
listened to local radio stations for news of potential detours I
might need to take. There were bridges out and large sections
of roads washed away. The covered bridge outside of Wildmont
had been completely demolished, and one of our local galleries
had been swept away by the normally docile Deerfield River. I
wanted to cry and wished I'd hear from Claude.

As Wildmont came into view, I could see fire trucks parked
across the road ahead. I drove toward them but detoured up
another road that eventually connected with Bartlet Mountain
Road.

Thoughts of Claude forced me forward.

Had he driven to the city?

He wouldn't do that without telling me.

My foot pressed harder on the gas. I knew I was driving too fast. The gravel road was heavily rutted from the runoff and soggy ground, but panic propelled me. My heart beat rapidly as I considered a life without Claude.

I had to find him.

The road was so uneven that my head nearly hit the roof of the cab as the truck bounced. I slammed on the brakes as I neared the turnoff for our road. The normally babbling stream running down the mountain had become a raging, red-brown torrent that had taken large sections of the road down the side of the mountain with it.

I shut off the truck and leapt onto the waterlogged road. The washed-away section was nearly five feet across. I knew it was a crazy idea, but I sprinted down the road away from the roaring gash. When I was about fifteen feet away, I turned and looked back toward the far edge.

You can make it. You can make it.

The ground's too wet; you won't have enough speed.

You can make it. You can make it.

I ran. My boots slipped at first, but soon found purchase. Time seemed to move differently. As if watching a movie in slow motion, I could see myself in the air and the raging water beneath me. It looked hungry as it dashed over rocks; tendrils and hands made of water seemed to reach up to pull me down, to take me with them as they raced down the mountain toward the river.

But they didn't get me. I slammed into the other side of the chasm, barely grasping the ground with my arms and torso. My boots dug in as I pulled myself up the other side. I stood and looked back at the truck. As I watched, another piece of the road tore away, widening the gap by an additional two feet.

I felt giddy; my muscles went slack with relief. For a split second, I forgot there was more to my mission. Then I remembered Claude, and the urgency of that thought obliterated any fatigue or slackness of muscle. I had to keep going on foot. I attacked the road that led up the mountain, taking large uphill steps. Some of the thin trees lining the way tore from the ground with the slightest tug. Others that I grabbed assisted me in my climb. The sound of the raging water taunted me, reminding me of dire possibilities. My boots slipped and sometimes sank into the earth, but nothing could keep me from reaching the first plateau where our house was situated.

When I finally rounded the curve, I looked down our short driveway. Only a ragged foundation and debris remained of the place where our house had stood. Claude's car sat askew, next to our decimated vegetable garden.

My knees buckled as shock and despair set in. *Was he in the house when it collapsed?*

My eye caught a flash of red flannel. A renewed energy spilled into me. I ran toward the house.

Please, please, I thought.

It was clear as I drew near: One of Claude's shirts was snagged in the pile of stones that used to be our fireplace. I pulled it free from the debris and held it up to my face, hoping to breathe in his scent, a mix of wood smoke, sandalwood soap and his skin.

I was too late. My vision blurred and all sound was sucked out of the world, as if a pillow had been wrapped around my head. My stomach lurched, but I had nothing to give but a dry heave. I stumbled forward, catching myself on a sharp rock.

This couldn't be the end. Wasn't it possible that he was hurt

and in need of help in the woods? I slowly walked the perimeter of the property, climbing over splintered timbers, broken
pieces of wood siding and smashed but recognizable pieces of
furniture. I peered down the hill into the woods. The roof had
sheared a tree in half and then caved in.

Could Claude be under there? I yelled his name, and a startled bird took flight from a nearby tree. The rapidly coursing
water relayed a dull roar, but there was no human response.

I'd walked back to the homesite, unsure where to go next,
when I heard the snap of a twig and a grunt. I looked beyond the
ruined garden and saw movement behind a stash of birches.

A tidal wave of relief crashed through me.

Claude emerged into the clearing, covered in mud from head
to toe, leaves and bits of branch clinging to his hair. I was so
overjoyed to see him that it took me a moment to realize that
rivulets of tears cut through the mud on his cheeks. His gaze
was on what he carried, and I recognized the equally muddy
body of Riley, limp in Claude's arms.

"Claude," I said softly.

He looked up at me, and his eyes widened with surprise.
"Oh, David, thank god. I couldn't call you. My phone was in
the house when it got washed away."

"I'm here now."

He walked into the foundation, toward me. He gently laid
Riley on the ground beside the fireplace. We sat beside him. I
reached out my hand and stroked his head. I was shocked when
he let out a long, low whine.

"He's alive?" I choked out.

"He's tired. I couldn't find any injuries, but we probably
should get him checked out." Claude looked at me, his expression tearful and guilty. "He ran off as I was packing the car
for West Coxsie. I should have gone after him right away, but I

thought he'd come back before it was time to go. He didn't, and I couldn't leave without him. I was supposed to protect him."

I slid closer to Claude and cupped his face in my hands. "So when the house went—"

"I was in the woods looking for him."

I tried not to imagine the two of them out in that weather and said, "He has a strong spirit. He'll be okay."

We stared into each other's eyes then embraced fiercely. Claude shook in my arms, overtaken by emotion, and we both began sobbing.

When we finally pulled apart, I opened my eyes. Even though our house was a chaotic pile of stone, jagged timbers and shattered glass, I'd never felt more at home.

"We've got a lot to rebuild."

NEW KID IN TOWN: 1977

Felice Picano

H ow good a party can it possibly be at four o'clock on a Sunday afternoon?"

"It's an L.A. party. You'll see," Andy responded. They were talking car to car, Andy of course having a car phone, too. Why didn't everyone?

"The only reason I would even dream of going," Vic admitted, "is that hot guy from New York who works for Long Meadow Records. He left a message at the hotel saying he'd be there. For him it's a work assignment."

"What guy? Is he cute?" Andy asked.

"You think I'd go all this way for a schmuck?"

"Speaking of schmucks…"

"Haven't seen his."

"Possibly you will today, since I expect this *soiree* will quickly devolve into an O-R-G-Y."

"At four in the afternoon? Tea and crumpets time?"

"It's a Hollywood *Hills* party, Vic. Wake up!"

"You 'expect?'—or you plan to *incite?*—an orgy?"

"Don't have to. The L_____ brothers will be there." Naming actors Vic had heard of—well, two of them. "All three will be present," Andy went on. "One L_____ brother among good-looking gay men is a certifiable orgy flint. Three of them? It might get out of hand."

"Good thing I wore clean underwear," Vic murmured then realized in an orgy it wouldn't stay on long. Maybe he should ink his name onto the back label when he disrobed, like parents did for their kindergartners' gloves and hats?

"It's not that far now," Andy insisted. "Only to Mount Olympus."

"Isn't that Northern Greece?"

"Try southern Laurel Canyon. Is that you in the pale-blue Caddy limo?"

"Why? Where are you?"

"Directly ahead. In the Sixty-three charcoal Lincoln Continental."

"You mean the one that looks like the Kennedy assassination vehicle?"

"*La même exactement!* Okay, that *is* you. I can see your lip gloss reflected in my mirror."

"Liar!"

"Twat! Have your driver follow me." Andy hung up.

"Meade, follow this guy ahead of us. The dark gray job," Vic specified. "He'll take us right to the house we're going to."

The phone rang again two minutes later: it was Vic's pal Gilbert in Manhattan.

As required, since Gilbert was his best friend, Vic reported the nearly sexual incident with the super good-looking room service waiter at the Beverly Hills Hotel.

"The waiter was probably just surprised by your openness,"

Gilbert opined. "He might be available. Be ready for him."

"Ready? What do I do if he says yes? Tip him when he arrives at five and comes at five-fifteen?"

"Depends how big *his* tip is!" Gilbert chortled. "Never mind: a fifty. Unless he reciprocates. Then at least a C-note."

"Gilbert, you see it now, don't you? It's all in some kind of perverted inverse ratio. The more disastrous the film business angle I'm involved in becomes, the more sex I seem to get out here."

"Inverse ratio? Oh you mean like, 'the angle of the dangle is equal to the heat of the meat?'"

"I go into any bar here on Santa Monica Bee and they're lined up, these amazing pretty boys in a row. Each of them ripe for the plucking by guess who? At this moment Andy is taking me to a Mount Olympus party he assures me will be a stupendous, star-studded orgy."

"You're never coming back, are you?" Gilbert asked.

"Last night before I'm to see Perfect Paul, fourth night in a row, there's this dinner party that Ed, the executive producer, is giving in his humongous, half-timbered castle somewhere in the Hills above the Sunset Strip. My driver is off for the latter part of the night, so I have them call a taxi to take me back to the hotel. Who shows up? Some twenty-four-year-old unemployed actor. Muscled. Darkly handsome. Green eyes. Thick, chestnut hair that falls like it's been ironed. Ratty surfer T-shirt that looks glued on with perspiration and jizz. Ditto for the ripped surfer shorts. Shorts and flip-flops, for chrissake, Gil! At night! Left nothing to the imagination."

"And we know that as an author you've got a great imagination. But...you're *about* to see Perfect Paul?" Gilbert reminded him.

"Exactly, so I'm shut-mouth quiet until we're two streets from the hotel on Sunset when Googie suddenly pulls over to the curb, stops, turns around and says could he ask me a question."

"No!"

"Honest to Grace Jones truth, Gilberto. So I say, ask away. Seems that a nice-looking, middle-aged fellow the night before gave Surfer-Dude Taxi-man a Cuban cigar as a tip and said he'd been thinking about what that cigar would look like in the driver's mouth the entire ride home."

"Shut! Up!"

"The Surfing Cabbie says he stripped off the cellophane and put the Cubano cigar in his mouth for the guy, who tipped him and got out."

"Uh-huh?" Even clever Gilbert couldn't see where this was going.

"So the cab driver gets all philosophical and asks, 'What do you think that was *really* about?'"

"You mean," Gilbert asked, "because Freud said sometimes a cigar is *just* a cigar?"

"Looking at this guy, Gillo, and how he was more and mostly *less* dressed, Freud does not at *all* apply. I was bored and a little *'stunada* from dinner's fourteen wines and I said the first thing that came into my mind. Which was, 'Your fare wanted you to blow him.'"

"You didn't!" Gil's voice rose two octaves.

"I was bored. I was high. What would *you* think?"

"I'd *think* it! I wouldn't say it."

"Well, I *said* it. 'Really?' Driver Googie asks, not at all offended. I said 'Really!' and then for verisimilitude, I added, 'Your fare probably was holding some other twenties in his hand, like this.' I splayed out my hand with three of them, one for the ride and two others."

"Oy! The writer and his verisimilitude," Gilbert groaned.

"And the Surfer-Dude says, 'He *was* holding them out. Just like that!'"

"Saints alive, Miss Sofonsiba!"

Vic went on. "Then I added, 'Which he wanted you to have. Or, I might be wrong, and instead, you being cute and all, maybe he wanted to blow *you*.'"

"Tell me you didn't actually say that, in the back of a cab on Sunset Boulevard and... Where were you?" Gilbert asked.

"I don't know. Foothill. Alpine. One of those cross streets. It was fascinating, Gilbert, watching all the counters tumbling around behind that perfect face like in a slot machine. I kept holding out the twenties at Sir Gidget the Hunky Cabbie, and suddenly all the counters fell into place going *blink blink blink* in those money-colored eyes. I swear I all but heard them go *ka-ching!* He snatched the twenties, stuffed them in his T-shirt pocket and said, 'Okay. But I gotta stay in the car in case I get a dispatch call.' So he drove up a block or two behind the hotel, hopped into the backseat and I had steak for the second time last night."

"All because...?" Gilbert hadn't quite gotten the *moral,* and he needed one for closure.

"All because I was about to meet Perfect Paul and didn't care if I sucked off this handsome, unemployed surfing actor's eight-incher. Ergo, I was casual enough about it for him not to be threatened in the least."

"You...are...the master of the hetero pick-up, Vic-tor-ee-a."

"I'm hanging up, Gil-berto."

"Go to the leather bar premiere!"

"I said no, Gilbert! No!" and Vic hung up. At which moment he realized he hadn't completely shut the window between the front and back, and his tall, ugly limo driver had heard every word.

After another minute or so they stopped and there was a tap on his side window. Andy. They'd arrived.

Now on his seventh day in town, Victor had ceased to be amazed by the interior décor of Los Angeles houses. Their sheer nuttiness was outdone only by their expense and by the fact that given the chance, he'd move in to any of them in a second.

This one, contemporary stone, steel and glass, was set in the woods, making it totally private; only the roof deck had a view. The house sported what L.A. people referred to as "various water features"—brooks, rills, little cascades, larger waterfalls and several pools, including the first infinity version he'd ever seen up close, as well as a lap pool, two hot tubs and several footbaths. They were all over the house on every level. Filled with hot guys frolicking—either naked or almost so in Speedos.

Since it actually was a business, or at least a publicity, event for some new Disco Diva discovery for Long Meadow Records, the entry and main rooms had the appurtenances of such, at least as Vic had come to know them: a long table set up with copies of her "fabulous new single" as well as an eight-minute, longer version for club deejays to spin, along with photos, bios and such. The Diva herself had already been there and was expected to return and sing a number after she made a surprise appearance at some club on The Strip for a "buncha business types."

And there Mark was, at the table, dressed in dark slacks, tan and black silk shirt and brown penny loafers. He looked professional. Vic had forgotten how manly, but not how handsome, he was.

Vic and Andy were greeted by their host—wet, not quite dripping, wrapped in a rainbow-colored bathrobe—along with Long Meadow Records' owner, a feisty little bulldog of a hot Jewish New York number named Hal Dern, who was also dripping but clad in only a Speedo with a two-sizes-too-small guinea A-shirt on top.

Andy took one look at Mark, whom he'd never met before, and said, "Honey, get those clothes off so we can see all your muscles. All of them, I say, child!"

He soon enough vanished arm in arm with the host, while Hal gave Vic a hug.

"The big man!" Hal announced as though there were two hundred and not six other people in the room. "The famous writer! Out in Hollywood making deals!"

"The big record producer!" Vic declaimed back. "The famous Star Maker! Out in Hollywood launching a Diva."

Having failed to embarrass Vic, Hal left muttering something.

"What'd he say?" Vic had to ask Mark.

"He's got some single-cut coke in his bedroom."

"I'll pass. Did you have any?"

"One line. Hours ago. So!" Mark looked pleased. "You showed up."

"You doubted?" Vic asked.

"I'd heard you were very busy. Working for some film company."

"If you call that work. But it looks like you really *are* working."

"I've got to stand here and greet everyone and offer them a disc and this material." He handed them to Vic and even put them in a shiny plastic bag for him.

"And you can't go into the water and show all those muscles, child!" Vic added.

"Not until six. Our flight is at seven-thirty. That gives me about..."

"Three minutes in the water."

"That's what I figured." Mark looked unhappy. "And I arrived yesterday morning on a red-eye. With Her in tow, and I mean in tow given her size and heft. And I was with her or setting this up all the rest of the time."

"And now you've got to go home. Doesn't sound like much fun."

"It's a job," Mark admitted.

"Where's Will?" Vic asked.

"Will?"

"Will Traylor?

"I guess back in New York. Why?"

Will had introduced them. Actually, Will had brought Vic to meet Mark one day at the offices of Long Meadow Records, talking about Mark in detailed, adoring length before and after said meeting.

"Nothing. I just got the impression he was...you two were..."

"Did Will tell you that?" Very sincere and concerned.

"Maybe I just assumed it."

"Oh?"

Maybe because Will wanted me to assume it? Vic thought. *Because Will knows I'd never bird-dog anyone he was dating.*

"It's not important," Vic said.

"But you came anyway?" Mark asked.

"I thought you'd want support...you know, a familiar face in a strange town..." Vic trailed off.

"You came out of loyalty?"

"I suppose."

"Not because of 'the guys?'" Mark pointed inside to where the action allegedly was.

"I just heard about 'the guys' while driving over here. Are all the rumors true?" Vic asked.

"How could I tell, stuck here in the foyer?"

Andy chose that moment to reappear. He was in small, square, Nautica boating shorts, and nothing else. He took Vic aside. "It's insane. In five minutes I've ingested two sizable loads of man-juice. When are you coming?"

"In a minute. I'm busy."

Andy looked over at Mark. "You've got the eye, my pal. He's a beaut." He sized up Mark, who was now talking to two new arrivals, and said, "Not quite a beer-can dick, but almost. You may not be able to handle it."

Vic laughed. "How could you possibly tell that through Dockers?"

"All the cock I've seen in my life, honey? Please! I'm a professional. Little secret: The giveaway is the guy's ass. The size, shape, but mostly the angle. His ass is good-sized and firm looking, already an important indicator for size given his waist is only about thirty inches. But see how his ass angles up, not down? That's because those upper glute muscles are needed to hold a larger male member than normal in front."

"Oh, please." Vic was blushing. "Even so, how do you know it's not long instead of thick?"

"That's where experience, and even more, instinct, come into play," Andy lectured.

"I'll bet."

"You'll see that I'm right."

Vic changed the topic. "Are the L_____ brothers here?"

"I thought I saw one. Maybe not." Andy then named three music stars he'd already encountered around the house in "embarrassing positions."

Vic would grant him two, but of the third: "Isn't he married to a famous bikini model?"

"All I know is he pushed me away from the two, I said *two*, large, tubular, fleshy objects he was taking turns having his way with. I'm going to have to let"—Andy named a British singer known to be fey—"who's holding court in the footbaths, do me. Just to tell everyone he did. Although he's done everyone else here, too. Toodles!"

Vic went into the other room and came back with a vodka tonic for himself and another Gerolsteiner bottled water for Mark.

"Thanks. I am stuck here."

"I'll take over if you need a men's room run. I've almost learned your *spiel* by heart."

"Very funny." Mark looked at Vic more seriously. "Look, I know that you're famous and all. But I've never read any of your books."

"The whippings begin at nine on the dot," Vic said darkly. "Of course if you read one of my books before then and can pass a simple, hundred-question, true or false quiz, you're safe."

"I'm not seeing Will," Mark said. "Nothing against him. I'm just not."

"Cool. Okay," Victor replied and suddenly felt that a door had just wedged open. "My next book is out in three months. Read that one. It's my best. Based on a historical incident in the Midwest around the turn of the century."

"I see people reading your books all the time. I'm just into other stuff. The *Ballets Russes*. I'm reading about Diaghilev now."

"The Russian impresario?"

"There's this new book out on him and Nijinsky. And another on Nazimova, the Twenties Russian film star."

"Rudolf Valentino's beard," Vic said. "I saw her film, *Salome.*"

"Wasn't that great!" Mark enthused. "Those art deco

costumes. Even when she was at rest, the feathered points of her crown were in wavelike motion all the time!"

And so in between new arrivals, they talked about Stravinsky and Ida Rubenstein, Debussy and Rimsky, Ravel and Lotte Lehmann.

Andy would reappear at intervals of fifteen minutes, with news flashes from the infinity pool or lower spa. "Took two more loads. While I was busy rimming a hot, shaved-head Brazilian named Emilio, one of the L_____ brothers suddenly began porking me! Without even asking my permission! Of course, once I saw who was halfway up my anal canal, I let him."

At a later check-in, Andy told them the married musician "is really going to hell. Coking, tripping *and* sucking. Super slut!"

By 4:30 the new arrivals were down to a trickle. By 4:45, they were nonexistent. Mark and Vic got chairs and fresh bottled water. They were comparing Beecham versus Toscanini's conducting style, and whether Gieseking or Michelangeli was *the* Beethoven pianist of the century, when the host came out in thrown-on street clothes, distress apparent in at least one small, relatively undrugged region of his face.

"Had to phone an EMT unit. Let me know when they arrive!"

"Someone almost drown?" Vic asked.

He named the model's hubby. "He's got killer cramps and is vomiting."

Five minutes later the emergency truck arrived, and Hal Dern appeared and gave minute-by-minute updates from the bedroom hallway as they pumped out the guy's stomach, installed a five-minute drip against dehydration, and then left.

One of the EMT guys came back and called for the host to sign some papers. Mark went to get him, leaving Vic alone with the med worker, a tall, red-bearded fellow.

"You seem pretty blasé about a near drowning," Vic said.

"Near drowning *in semen,* you mean! I'm blasé because it happens once a month."

"You're kidding."

"At least. Hetero amateurs!" The med worker sneered. "They all want to take a walk on the wild side. Think it's so cool. Tomorrow night they'll tell all their friends at the dinner table how they starred at a homo bash. They don't realize a guy's jizz is chock-full of amino acids. Different acids for different guys. If you're not used to them..."

Luckily, Andy *was* used to them, given the rate he was going today.

When Mark arrived, the med worker said, in a voice only they could hear, "Look, the homeowner and that other guy are busy partying. You two look sober and responsible. You ought to get this guy," meaning the rock star, "back to where he lives. Drive him. Give him these if he gets woozy in the car." He handed over some Dramamine. "Can I count on you?"

"Don't worry," Mark assured him.

"I've got a car and driver," Vic said.

"Good men! Go in half an hour at the latest," the med worker said. "I put a sedative in his drip. He'll be going under."

"There goes your three minutes in the pool," Vic said when the EMT guy left. "Why not get your bags and all, we'll drive this guy home and then I'll have my driver take you right to the airport?"

Andy came out to report that the gay Brit tenor gave passable head, but "nothing to sing about." And that it was rumored that someone famous had overdosed.

"Everyone's fine," Mark said, trying to dampen the rumor.

Meade, Vic's limo driver, helped them with the singer, getting him out to the Caddy without anyone else seeing. The rock star looked short, thin and craggy, exhausted, pale and already very drowsy. Vic's driver surprised them by saying, "I know where he lives. Took them home from an event once," emphasizing the word *them*.

In the backseat of the car, the rock star fell asleep sloppily, first on Vic's shoulder, and then when he moved him gently to the seat, onto Mark's chest. Mark let him lean against him. What a nice guy.

Mark and the driver half carried the rock star up the few stairs and into the foyer. A blonde in yoga togs and a Mexican housekeeper, both of whom seemed concerned, answered their ringing.

Meade remained talking with the wife a moment after Mark had left and wrote something down on a piece of paper for her.

"I left your name and your hotel number," he reported to Vic when he returned to the driver's seat. "Just in case he's a good guy."

"Come on! He'll be too embarrassed."

"Well, I wrote it anyway," Meade said.

Traffic was easy going west, and Mark relaxed for the first time and shut his eyes. Vic let him lean on his shoulder, not minding the pressure one bit. He thought Mark was dead asleep until Meade announced they were at LAX and asked what airline they needed. That was when Mark took Vic's hand in his and answered the driver. Vic couldn't believe how oddly exciting that moment was, suddenly feeling his hand clasped so—affectionately? proprietarily?—in Mark's hand. And Mark held it until the car stopped for him to get out.

"You're on time! As promised," Vic said when they were at the car's trunk, getting Mark's luggage. Mark kept looking at him, so Vic asked, "What?"

"In New York? Two weeks from now—you'll be back by then, right? There's a performance at Lincoln Center: a double bill of Stravinsky's Octet and *L'Histoire du Soldat* in English. They're very seldom done." He named a well-known English actor who would narrate the latter chamber opera.

"Okay. Sure, I'll go with you."

Vic wrote down his phone number for Mark, who put it into his shirt pocket by his heart.

Meade went to park the limo. Vic walked Mark to his plane and waited with him in the departure lounge. When his seating section was called, Mark hugged him quickly, hard, so that Vic was suddenly enfolded within the strong, solidity of his arms, shoulders and upper back. Vic felt the oddest little flutter in his chest.

Mark stepped away without another word and without looking back.

Still unhinged by that little flutter that he'd felt only once before in his life, over a decade before, Vic waited until, from the floor-to-ceiling departure lounge glass, he could see Mark's 707 taxi. It ascended safely into the air and stashed itself inside LAX's perpetual clouds.

I'm just a hopeless romantic, Vic told himself. *Here I go again!*

In the car, Meade commented, "He seemed like a together guy."

"He did, didn't he?" Vic responded.

He was amazed by the entire crazy, and he supposed typically gay, Hollywood afternoon. All these months he'd been waiting for the future to open up for him in California. Instead, he had a date he was looking forward to in New York with Mark. And who knew what else?

THE GREEN SWEATER

Mark G. Harris

The big gabled and gazeboed house on Berrynook Avenue was old. A glance at the clock revealed that the night wasn't much of a toddler, either. However, the party inside the house seemed to have only just hit puberty.

A drag queen, who preferred to keep it a secret that her real name was Logan Strongosky, tripped over empty beer bottles left with greatest courtesy on the staircase. She was assisted to the upright position by a leather dom who told very few that his driver's license displayed the name Myron Fultz. They both paused to wave at the young man responsible for the set decorations and painted backdrops from the performance earlier that evening. Jay nodded his winning chin back at them as he squeezed between the theater majors gathered around the piano and tried to get to the bathroom.

The bathroom tucked underneath the stairs was occupied. Tiptoeing around the empties, Jay went upstairs and discovered two girls from rival softball teams, an accountant, and a furniture mover all seated on the rim of the bathtub. They were sampling from a couple of bottles of wine while their toes tested the water. In spite of his urgency, Jay lighted a cigarette for a girl who couldn't seem to manage the act on her own. He squandered an excruciating thirty seconds answering the furniture mover's fumbled knock-knock joke. He excused himself to try his luck with the downstairs john again. It was available now, and the call of nature, its light blinking on line one, was heeded—not a moment too soon.

Jay washed his hands and contemplated his luck. He didn't have a conceited bone in his body. To his mind, it wasn't the magnetism of a winning chin, but more likely a kind shove of luck that had propelled him into sublime collision with Doug tonight. No other power besides luck could have dropped Jay within kissing distance of the golden lump of that Adam's apple above the silk purple knot of Doug's safety-pins-studded necktie. They'd hit it off. An hour's conversation was sufficient to make Jay want to mate socks with Doug at a Laundromat years from now. He wanted to steal bacon off of Doug's breakfast tray. Though modest, Jay was in love with the unfolding idea of Doug and himself getting immodest. He corrected himself; he was in lust with the idea and hoped it might unfold days from now, instead of years, but he was prepared to wait it out.

Jay's laryngeal musings at the sink might have continued to curlicue unchecked had he not discovered something.

Beside the soap dish stood a folded piece of paper, arched like the roof of a house, or a sawhorse or a displeased eyebrow. It read, *HELP ME!*

He opened the note.

If you are reading this you have to help me. This boring guy who is really, really stupid has latched on

to me and WILL NOT LEAVE ME ALONE. I'm
at this party on my own. I don't know anybody, so
you have to come up to me and pretend you know
me and RESCUE ME FROM THIS FREAK. I need
a ride home, too. You can't miss me. I'm the VERY
CUTE BOY being tortured by the JERKOFF in the
GREEN SWEATER.

Jay placed the note against his chest and examined the hole he'd just noticed in his sweater, near the collar. He also noted, as if seeing it for the first time, that his sweater was the jarring, unnatural color of TV-dinner peas, or golf courses in wintertime.

"So…" Jay said, not really knowing where to go with the word.

The invitation to this party hadn't specified a dress code. The female impersonator and the dungeon master could have attested to that, were they not so busy discussing the process of legally changing one's name over the hors d'oeuvres platter. If nothing else, the group upstairs in the bathtub brought new clarity to the old saying, "Less is more." But for those conscious of their appearances, it went without saying that one should pay at least a little attention to what is worn to a party. It went without being said, though it probably should have been shouted at Jay.

He'd put on the sweater tonight because it was his favorite, his security, his old reliable. He never stirred a hot cup of cocoa without wearing the sweater, if he could help it. It protected his forearms, when he was working, from stray droplets of paint. Maybe its color wasn't the most flattering shade he could have chosen. Maybe the time to retire it was overdue, a time all holey, acrylic-splattered knitwear must face. Maybe the sweater was to blame for making a guy Jay liked, who he thought liked him, desperate to escape. Jay was ready to blame the sweater, to blame anything but himself, for causing someone to call him "boring," and "really, really stupid."

"You," he said to his reflection, "are only marginally stupid. Your sweater might be threadbare, but at least you washed it...recently. Face it, you're a catch." Though his bones passed muster, Jay had a conceited knuckle or two.

Over his head, Jay heard the bump and thud of someone coming to grief on the staircase and was brought back, realizing he'd hogged the bathroom long enough. He put the note back where he'd found it and unlocked the door. Then he froze. He snatched the note and pocketed it. The note needn't be seen by anybody else. The note's author would need no rescuer, either. Jay would do the honors and make himself, and his offensive sweater, scarce.

Jay's friend Vince flagged him down in the hallway, which was nearly impassable with partying and necking.

"Jay-ronimo!"

Jay stared through him for a moment, until recognition set in. "Vince. Yeah, hi."

Vince rubbed Jay's cheek. "Drinking much?"

"Not enough. Still don't want to go to bed with you." The rub became a smack. "God, that's good."

"Not sure you could handle sleeping with me." Vince smiled. "Where's that dude you've been talking to all night while you've been forgetting I exist?"

Jay closed his eyes. "Him, hmm. His status has been upgraded to Up For Grabs, if you feel like going for it."

"He is sort of on the tasty side. Salty little urban fantasy."

"Actually he's really—" Jay was on the verge of saying the word *nice*, or in some other way conveying to Vince that Doug had even more going for him than his dudeitude. The note in his pocket made him rethink, as well as crumple. He stroked the back of Vince's neck. "Funny you should mention it. What I've been fantasizing about is you fetching me a bottle of beer."

"Excuse me?"

"See, there's this ice chest. Sitting on the island in the kitchen. Filled with beers. You follow?" Jay's thumb and forefinger strayed to rub the tiny ruby in Vince's left earlobe.

"That tickles." Vince jerked his head aside. "Go get it yourself. You're a big boy. That's not exactly what the stories circulating about you have to say about it, but you know what I mean. I'm going to go and charm your little friend."

Vince sandwiched himself farther into the hallway's throng, while Jay opted for the scenic living-room-to-kitchen route. Vince called out, before they lost each other's visuals, "Jay! What's that dude's name, anyway?"

"It's—Larry!"

Jay's heart mumbled a numb beat in a chest-deep bath of disappointment as he forced himself through the living room's gridlock. Autopilot helped him maneuver. He didn't see. He didn't register the pretty girl singing. The drama students were hoisting her onto the piano, though he didn't notice them. He had no eyes for the pretty boy who yawned and nodded on the sofa, and no eyes for the boy's companion, busy adjusting the sleeves of his olive drab cardigan around his shoulders to fashion a preppy cape. Jay had eyes only for a bottle of beer from the kitchen. He rescued one from a tragic ice-chest drowning. He turned and headed for the front porch. It amazed him that he ended up finding it—amazed since he could see only a smeared and shimmering image of a stillborn future with Doug.

"Doug," Jay said. "Thought you liked me, Doug." He liked saying that name. It was one of those words with requirements, formed more with the throat than the lips. Though the lips were invited, too.

He sat on the top step, spread his legs in a relaxing divide, and twisted off the beer's cap. No one else shared the porch with him, and he considered chucking the bottle cap into the bushes. He placed it inside his pocket instead, to help the environment and to keep the note company. Behind him, the front door opened. Then it closed. Footsteps approached Jay's rear.

"Okay, I give up. Why can't an elephant ride a tricycle?" Doug sat next to him.

Though Jay had skateboarded his way into an emergency room bill or two in his day, he felt certain that seeing Doug again topped any garish injury of which he'd ever been proud in terms of eye-openers. This topped them all without lube. "Huh?"

Doug nudged Jay's shoulder with his. "Your joke. You said you'd tell me the punch line when you got back. Why'd you come out here, anyway?"

Somebody was trying to win the coveted Medal for Outstanding Politeness tonight. Jay had at times made a play for it himself, like when he'd been invited by Vince's family to share Thanksgiving with them two weeks ago. Though Vince's mother could cook about as well as Jay could do fractions, he'd grimaced at her and asked for second helpings.

Rather than telling Doug he was on to him, Jay manufactured a smile. "Somebody around here has to be the lookout. Any minute this party's going to bring down the law. Why'd you come out here?"

"Besides looking for you?"

This guy was unbelievable. He was bypassing Outstanding Politeness and bucking for the Nobel Two-Faced Prize. "Yeah," Jay said, "besides looking for me."

"I don't know." Doug tucked his hands into the armpits of his shirt and hunched his shoulders around his ears. "Every time I go to a party, I like to step away from it for a minute, you know? Mentally photograph it. I like to look at all of the people, like here tonight, and wonder where they'll be in ten years' time. You, you'll probably be going after an art career in New York, won't you?"

Jay twisted the bottle in his hands. "I'm staying in town, buying a little house, getting old and crotchety, whatever that means, and selling my designed skateboards on eBay. Or maybe studying to become a tattoo artist. I haven't made up my mind."

When Doug failed to laugh at these future endeavors, Jay came within perilous proximity of hugging him. No one had ever listened to Jay's plans without offering them a smidgen of ridicule.

"That's weird," Doug said.

Jay's urge to hug him flatlined. "What's so weird about it?"

"All of my plans include growing old, too."

The beer in Jay's hands was easier to figure out than anything else he'd been exposed to tonight, so he rewarded it by giving its rim a gentle, receiving kiss.

Doug shivered.

"Cold?"

"A little."

"You could go back inside," Jay said.

"Or I could stay out here. With you."

Jay stared at his beer, thanking it, despite having no telepathic energy, for not harassing him with confusion, for being cold and tasty and simple. "Where's your coat?"

"This girl inside took a shine to it. Last I saw, she was reenacting that bullet dodging scene from *The Matrix*." He looked at Jay with what seemed to be a sated reassurance. He smiled. He made no move to leave Jay's side in search of other warmth.

In the arena of Jay's head, the words *boring* and *freak* and *really, really stupid* played out a gruesome conflict against the look Doug was giving him.

If, in ten years' time, this moment were only a photograph, Jay knew he would long only to lean closer and touch the paper with his nose. When, tomorrow, Doug ceased to be in Jay's life, to remain only a remembered word, Jay wanted his throat alone to be the one lucky enough to hug the spoken name. But right now, he yearned to cradle his head between Doug's shoulder and neck and feel the young man's Adam's apple throb next to his forehead in speech. Jay knew how Doug disliked him, and he knew that this last desire wasn't possible, and he became a little older and a little sadder for it. But he took off his sweater.

The lyrics in love songs might have made sense to some and might not have made sense to others. Jay felt something wholly hopeless and senseless struggle within him. It only made sense if he were in love. If Jay were not in love, then he knew that he wasn't made to make sense, that sense was to be used by lesser beings, particularly common sense.

Though the evidence that he wasn't welcome to embrace Doug was wadded up in his pocket, Jay handed him the green sweater, enjoying the thought that at least the sweater could surround Doug in his arms' stead and keep Doug warm. The world was peopled with heroes who left their most sensitive part vulnerable and offered over their armor with a resigned expectation of the fatal wound and without a hope of reprieve. Even on Berrynook Avenue, the heroic could happen.

Aside from grinding down the railing of that long flight of stairs behind the Community Theater, giving Doug his sweater was, to date, the most adventurous thing that Jay had ever done.

Jay turned away. He took a swig of his beer. He watched

a taxicab pull into the driveway. In his periphery, he saw that Doug still hadn't put on the sweater. "It's been flea-dipped, you know? You don't have to worry. Besides, the green will look good with your purple tie. Purple and green look good together. They like each oth—"

"I was right about you."

Jay faced him. "Right about what?"

"I had you pegged for gallantry from the moment you called going to the bathroom 'using the facilities.'"

"I never said that."

"Yes, you did."

"Did I?"

"Anyway, what about you? Aren't you cold?"

Jay freed a hand from beer duty and extended it to Doug. "Feel it."

Doug's hand slipped into Jay's. "God. It's like a heater."

"There's another one where that came from." Jay frowned at his forwardness. "Sorry."

Doug laughed. "Why are you sor—"

Behind them the door opened, and a pretty, though crabapple-faced, boy walked across the porch to the steps. "Could you get out of my way, please?" he said to Jay. Jay scuttled closer to Doug.

Behind the boy, a man loitered in the doorway. "So, okay, you've got my number. See you tomorrow night."

"You bet," the boy said, not looking back. He rolled his eyes at Jay as he moved past him.

"Get home safe," the man called and turned to go back inside.

Jay saw the color of the sweater draped on the man's back just before the man reentered the house. The front door shut. He heard the boy in the driveway telling the cabdriver, "I've never been so glad to see a taxi in my life. Ugh!" He watched the boy board the backseat and slam the door. He waited until the taxi backed out of the driveway, waiting for what he couldn't say. And he felt Doug's hand, still clasping his.

Rather than contemplate his luck any further, Jay wondered why he'd ever felt the need for any armor, any security. Inside his chest, his busy blood-pump took on an added assignment with great eagerness.

Doug released Jay's hand. He pulled himself, murmuring, into Jay's sweater, while Jay watched him with a renewed appreciation for every single thing under the moon.

"You got anything planned day after tomorrow?" Doug asked.

Jay shook his head.

"That's good."

"Why is that good?"

"Because," Doug hesitated and then laid his head on Jay's shoulder, "my roommate and I are going to hang some pictures in our apartment. We could use an artist's eye. Plus I'm making spaghetti carbonara, and we'll have plenty of—what is that you're drinking?"

"A Heineken."

"We'll have all the Heinekens you can stand."

"Carbonara, that's the one with bacon in it, isn't it?"

"Yeah."

Jay sighed. Although bacon was notorious for making him sigh, the escaped emotion may have been triggered by the pleasant sensation weighing, just right, on his healed and happy collarbone fracture.

"Can I bring a friend? I owe him a meal."

"Sure," Doug said.

"My artist's eye is all yours, then. There's another one where that came from, and this time I'm not sorry. I'll even hammer the nails for you."

"What makes you think I'm not the one who likes to do the hammering?"

"Oh, no—no. Everything was finally going so perfect. Why'd you have to go and say that?"

Doug nuzzled his cheek against Jay's shirt. "We've got time to iron that one out."

Jay thought it over and decided to say the word anyway. "Years. If you're up for it."

"And you don't have to be sorry. You don't have to be funny, either. You're not very good at it, you know?"

Jay put his arm around Doug and pinched the tip of Doug's nose. "How would you know? Unless wearing safety pins on a necktie makes you a good judge of humor."

"You never told me the punch line to your joke."

Leaning in for a kiss, Jay said, "Because his finger's too big to ring the little bell," and thrilled to the feeling of Doug's laughter filling his mouth.

ROCHESTER SUMMERS

Craig Cotter

I have only one photograph of Alex left: he's standing behind the cash register of Sunflower Pool. His brother John is there, too. I'm in the chemical section. I can see Alex from the side. He's wearing jeans, a T-shirt and a light spring coat. He stretches out over the counter and half his forearms show from the sleeves of the jacket—he has grown out of it. Dirty blond hair covers his ears.

That was in 1976. My parents wanted me to get a job and were talking to our neighbor, Mr. Glasser. He was part owner of Sunflower Pool and hired me to pour chlorine. The chlorine shed was in a back building. A two-hundred-gallon plastic tank of liquid chlorine came to a spigot. I'd turn it on, and it would fill a trough. I had four siphons. I dipped the siphons into the chlorine to get them going. I'd fill four gallon-jugs at a time, put four of the gallons together in a plastic crate and then stack them on a wood skid. When the skid was full—sixteen crates of chlorine stacked four deep—I'd get the forklift out of the loading dock, drive it over to the chlorine, pick up the skid and drive it up the hill to the front of the store.

One time the trough broke and flooded the shack with chlorine up to my ankles. I was wearing low-top Converse All-Stars (we didn't call them Chuck Taylors). All the cloth dissolved immediately. Only the rubber soles, the rubber toe area of the shoes and the metal eyelets were left. I drove home barefooted to get another pair of tennis shoes.

I was sixteen that summer. My dad, a General Motors carburetor engineer, had been transferred from Drayton Plains, Michigan, where I'd been since 1963—I'd grown up there. He was sent back to the mother ship, Rochester Products, the carburetor division of GM in Rochester, New York, the city where I was born.

All my friends lived in Michigan. I didn't know I was gay then. I tried to date a few girls. I knew that *fags* and *cocksuckers,* and anyone called those names in the assembly-line neighborhood I grew up in, got beaten up. Even though I dreamed of the paperboy, who was twelve when I was nine—daydreamed about him, too—I knew the whole getting-beat-up thing was no good.

There was a Victorian insane asylum in Pontiac, built in 1878—I'd see the spires every time my mom drove us out of the Pontiac Mall. We heard the fag kids went there for shock treatments.

I tried to cover. I got decent at sports. I was a catcher in baseball. I liked catcher because I got to put on all the equipment: mask, chest and leg protectors. Not many boys wanted to be catcher—in fact no one in my neighborhood wanted the job. You got hit with bats, balls and runners. I liked it—it kept me from being a fag.

* * *

I hated Rochester when we moved there. We lived in a condo in a suburb called Greece while our new house was being built a mile south of Lake Ontario. Greece was mostly farmland that was being slowly converted to housing subdivisions.

On a dark morning in early September—cold already—I waited at my bus stop. A boy my age, or maybe a year older, was already there. He was lean with dark curly hair. I said, "Hey." He didn't speak to me that morning or any other. I had a crush on him but didn't know it. He knew it. He slipped a death-threat note to me under my dad's windshield wiper. My dad told me to be careful about the boy.

"What did the note say?" I asked.

"It doesn't matter. He's not a good person."

My first year at the new high school totally sucked. I made the varsity baseball team, but once the season started, I couldn't hit anything. I'd lost my confidence.

That summer my dad bought me a 1969 Monte Carlo, gold with a black vinyl top. It had a V-8 engine. Got twelve miles per gallon. It was a two-door, bench seats front and back. I loved how the engine roared. Each day on my drive to Sunflower Pool I took the Parkway, a highway that ran along the south shore of Lake Ontario. Each day I'd push the speed up a bit. The car was stable at 110. Then it started to shimmy a bit. Like the wheels weren't entirely on the road. Like it was drifting and floating.

After pouring a skid of chlorine, I walked into the loading dock to get the forklift. To my right was a pump shop. There was a boy working there, standing with his back to me at his workbench. He was fifteen and a couple of inches taller than me. He was skinny with long fingers that were strong. His hands were much bigger than mine. That was Alex.

* * *

Alex became my first friend in Rochester. He turned around one day as I was getting the forklift and watched me. I looked at him and drove the lift out.

He asked me for a ride home that night. His brother John had driven him to work earlier and then left to pick up his girl-friend.

When the store was locked up, I got in my car and waited for Alex. My whole body ached from eight hours of pouring skids of chlorine. I played the FM radio and drank a Coke from a six-ounce bottle sold in the store's Coke machine.

Alex walked out of the shop toward my car. He was drinking a Coke, too. He moved fast and smooth, with big strides of his long legs. His straight bottom jeans were 28/34s. They still sagged on his hips.

He got in my car, and I wondered how I'd find my way back to the condo in Greece if I took him home. I knew only one way to work and didn't know the Rochester roads.

The Stones' "Angie" was playing.

"Eye-and-Jay," Alex sang.

I turned down the radio.

"You want to get something to eat?" he asked.

"Sure." I drove up the hill and stopped where the driveway met the street.

"Turn left," he said.

We ended up at Don & Bob's, a diner with stainless steel walls on a road that ran along Lake Ontario. We ordered cheeseburgers, fries and Cokes. Alex held his burger in his right hand—his fingers were longer than the bun. He shoveled in a third of the burger until it puffed up his cheeks. Then he jammed in five fries with his left hand. His meal was done in two minutes.

Later he directed me to his parents' house. On the drive, he told me about his high school; I told him about Michigan. When I pulled into his driveway, he hopped out and headed toward his parents' covered porch.

"How do I get home?" I called.

He came back and leaned in the passenger window. After giving me directions I wasn't sure I could follow, he said, "You working tomorrow?"

"Yeah."

He turned around and went inside.

I wore T-shirts and jean shorts to work all that summer. They were made from cut jeans, so the edges were frayed. The style was to cut them short. Way short. If I sat down you could see my balls in my jockey shorts.

On the days our shifts ended at the same time, I drove while Alex showed me different parts of Rochester. He'd ask me every day what time I was scheduled to get off then tell his brother that he didn't need a ride.

One night Alex pointed and said, "Turn there." We drove to a parking lot at the lake that held cars only one deep. Logs lined the lot so you wouldn't drive into the water.

He didn't ask me if I wanted to go swimming. It was eleven at night, a warm and muggy Rochester summer evening. We walked down to the rocky beach. I didn't know how to swim so I sat on a rock. He pulled off his T-shirt and threw it aside. He pulled off his tennis shoes and socks. He pulled off his jeans and threw them at me hard. I caught most of them, though one leg hit me on the side of the head. He threw his white briefs on some other rocks, ran five big strides to the lake, and dove in. He swam straight out. I lost sight of him after four strokes.

A half hour passed. Every five minutes I got more nervous.

I wasn't going to leave. I thought something was wrong. Waves hit the shore rocks. Then I saw his chest lift out of the water and slide back down.

He walked up and said, "Give me your shirt."

"Yours is over there."

"I'm freezing. Give me your shirt." I took off my T-shirt and gave it to him. He wiped himself down with it, threw it back to me and got dressed. I put my mostly wet shirt back on.

I liked Alex's older brother John. He was cool at work. He accepted me like Alex did. They weren't like the kids at my high school. John was two years older than Alex, just as tall, but a bit thicker. He wasn't fat—just thicker muscles, where Alex was all wiry.

Not long after Alex and I began hanging out, John walked up to me when I was getting a Coke out of the machine.

"I just want you to know Alex is gay," he said.

I didn't smile. I didn't say a word. I took a gulp of Coke, looked at John, and walked back to the water testing station. When we got out of work, Alex said he wanted to try Chinese food. We drove around looking for a Chinese restaurant. We found one by Kodak. We both liked it a lot. We decided that night never to eat at McDonald's again.

On my third week at Sunflower Pool, Alex and I were told to go upstairs to the warehouse to sort the shelves and do inventory.

The second-floor warehouse had floor-to-ceiling wood shelves ten feet tall. There were two large doors that led to a freight elevator.

"Be quiet," Alex said. "Check this out."

He picked up a pellet gun that was propped near the double doors. He slowly opened one door. Across from us was a ledge just under the roof of the cinderblock building. A line of five pigeons cooed on the ledge.

"They shit on everything," he said and handed me the gun.

I aimed at a pigeon that was six feet away. I hit it in the breast. There was a small puff of feathers and the pigeon dropped off the ledge and straight down into an open dumpster. The pellet gun was so quiet that it didn't bother the other four pigeons still sitting there. Alex took the gun from me and aimed, but the hollow lead pellet splatted against the cinderblock between two of the pigeons, making enough noise that all four birds took off.

Two hours later our T-shirts were soaked with sweat. We took them off and put them on a shelf. Some of the boxes were large swimming pool covers, too big for one person to move. We moved them together. Alex's torso had a thin coating of sweat. When we lifted boxes together, I could smell his armpits. When we were done, he put on my shirt and walked down the stairs to the showroom. I put on his and liked the smell of it. No one noticed we'd swapped shirts.

It was just a summer job for me, and I was only allowed to use the car when I was working. Alex was too young to have a car. That meant we couldn't see each other until the following summer, June of 1977. I'd turned seventeen and was still five feet, nine inches, but Alex, now sixteen, had grown an inch and was six feet tall. He was as skinny as ever. His forehead was a bit oily, and he had a couple of red zits.

After our first shift together, when I drove him home, he said, "You wanna see my room?"

Alex's family was German. His father had been a Hitler Youth. As a boy his dad was forced to defend Berlin with old men, as all the soldiers from eighteen to sixty were dead or in

POW camps. An artillery shell hit a hundred feet from his father, at the time a twelve-year-old boy. His only injury was that his head no longer sat upright on his shoulders. It leaned slightly to the left side. His kids called him "Lop" behind his back.

Alex had two sisters and two brothers. Only one brother was younger; all the other kids were older. They lived in a two-story house with a full attic and full basement. Alex had his own room. It had high ceilings and hardwood floors.

I wore jeans that were 28/34 like Alex, but I rolled my cuffs. Alex opened his closet and told me to take a pair of his jeans.

"What for?"

"I'm going to wear yours."

He pulled a pair of worn and faded jeans off a hanger and handed them to me. I turned away from him, facing the open closet, and took off my jeans. I then put on his. I sat down on his bed. Facing me, he took off his jeans, took mine off the floor and put them on.

For the rest of the summer, we traded clothes. Every time he came to my house, he'd strip to his jockeys and grab what he wanted out of my closet and out of my drawers. Socks, too, and sometimes underwear.

One day when he was going through my drawers he found a pair of white socks and told me to wear them.

"I don't like socks," I told him.

"Wear them today and tomorrow to work."

I did it. When I drove him home, he pulled off his shoes in my car, took off his socks, told me to give him mine, and to wear his.

I never put Alex's clothes in the laundry hamper at home. My mom knew we swapped clothes in my bedroom, but she never said anything. I thought as long as I didn't put Alex's clothes in the wash, she probably wouldn't.

That summer and the next, every week that we worked together, we traded clothes. After that first summer, I took his clothes only after he'd worn them for a couple of days without washing them. I could smell Alex's legs in his jeans. I liked the smell of his armpits in his T-shirts.

We never talked about it.

Alex's favorite album was Supertramp's *Breakfast In America*. My favorite bands were the Beatles and the Rolling Stones. We'd take turns putting cassettes in my car stereo. I didn't think Supertramp was very good and tried to explain why. I said some of the lyrics were "clichés."

We saw on a magazine that Mick Jagger had a diamond in his front tooth and decided we wanted one. The dentist we went to said it wasn't a good idea. I had the magazine cover of Mick in my pocket and showed it to the dentist. He said he'd have to file down a tooth, and then put the diamond in a crown. We said, okay, how much? The dentist refused to file down our healthy teeth. We thought he was a dickhead but gave up the plan and decided to get our ears pierced instead. We split the pair of studs they give you when they pierce your ear. They were blue rhinestones.

The summer after I graduated from high school, Alex's aunt, who he called *Tante* Martha, gave him her car, a 1967 Rambler: four-door, powder blue. He decided to learn how to paint a car: got a book, sanded the body down, filled in the dents, and got a car paint sprayer. This took many hours over the summer.

I borrowed my dad's Nikon, a thirty-five millimeter, and took twelve rolls of black-and-white photographs of Alex as he worked on the Rambler. He never minded getting his picture taken. He never smiled for the camera—though sometimes he looked directly in it—or into my eyes at the viewfinder. I got him from all angles, shirt on and off.

I'd been accepted to Michigan State and was moving to East Lansing in the fall. Alex didn't like high school and was thinking of dropping out. He wanted to get a pickup truck and start his own business. He'd build swimming pools and service them.

One August night after work, Alex directed me to Hamlin Beach State Park. It was on the coast of Lake Ontario about twenty miles west of Rochester. When we got there, a wooden parking arm blocked the entrance at the stone guardhouse.

"They can't close the beach," I said. "It's state land; we all own it."

I drove around the wooden arm. Alex directed me to the far west parking lot near sand cliffs. We parked the car and walked up a hill. The grass stopped and there was a barbed-wire fence with NO TRESPASSING signs on it. Behind the fence were woods. Alex showed me a place where the fence had been pushed down. We stepped over it and onto a sand path.

We walked about a hundred yards out to a bluff forty feet above the beach. The roots of all the trees near the edge of the cliff dangled in the air. I sat on the edge. Alex sat behind me. He wrapped his legs around mine and put his arms around me. We didn't talk. His flat stomach was against my back. I leaned my head into his chest.

After a couple of hours, cones of many-colored lights descended from the sky. They pulsed. We had no idea what was going on. We didn't know they were the Northern Lights.

When we walked down the cliff to the parking lot around three in the morning, my car was gone. We walked miles to find a pay phone and called the police. They'd towed my car.

It was a huge amount of money to get my car out of impound.

Instead of paying the fine, I went to court in Hamlin to make my case that the beach shouldn't be closed at night. The judge yelled at me, doubled the fine and told me to get out of his town.

The next time we had a night off together, we drove around the guardhouse again but hid my car in the trees. The Northern Lights weren't out, but we sat on the cliff edge in the same way, not talking for hours.

I wrote Alex a letter every month my freshman year. He wrote back only once, with green ink on lined paper. I still have that letter.

Three summers later, when Alex told me he was getting married to a girl, I looked through the 144 photos of him again and threw them all away—negatives, too. I haven't made too many mistakes in my life—but that's one of my bad ones. I got him so clear and so young. Alex had a great face: wide, with high cheekbones, full lips, honest eyes.

I still dream about those photos.

BOTHERED, BEWILDERED

Rob Williams

I was eleven when I told my ten-year-old neighbor that I was a witch. Or a warlock, I should say, since guys can't be witches. Chalk it up to too many reruns of "Bewitched" on television. I told Jimmy I was friends with Samantha, Endora and Doctor Bombay.

"They're just a TV show," he said, squinting with skepticism, so that the tiny wrinkles around his eyes, not unusual for a California kid, deepened.

"Not those people," I replied. "Those are actors, acting out the real witches' lives. I'm talking about the real Samantha, the real Endora, the real Doctor Bombay."

Jimmy had the whitest-blond hair of any kid I'd ever seen. In summer it turned green from all the chlorine in his family's pool, where we would swim unsupervised for hours, sometimes even days. I told him that the green hair meant he had the potential to be a warlock, too. I would be like his Jedi Master, teaching him his craft.

* * *

How I proved to Jimmy that I was a warlock (the first time):

We were one of the first families on our block to get a Clapper—a device that turns a lamp on and off when you clap. It was plugged in behind the end table in our living room next to the couch my grandmother called the *davenport*. I showed the lamp trick to Jimmy. Clapped it on and off. His eyes grew wide, his mouth open, lips shiny with spit. I clapped it on and off again. Told him I would transfer my power to him so he could do it. He ate it up—clapping hesitantly at first. I was surprised it went on. Then he clapped harder. Clapped that lamp on and off, off and on, for twenty minutes. I thought his hands would fall off. We played Atari, and every couple of minutes he would clap the lamp on or off and smile that stupid smile. When he went to take a pee, I turned off the Clapper so it became just a regular lamp. Jimmy came back and tried to clap it on again. It didn't turn on. He clapped again harder. He clapped close to the lamp, right above the lamp, below it; still nothing.

"Don't abuse the power," I said.

How I proved to Jimmy that I was a warlock (the second time):

Two words—*Sea Monkeys*.

"Being a warlock," I told him, "means you have the power to create life. Whole villages in fact."

I dumped that packet of crystallized brine shrimp into the jar of water and stirred vigorously, and soon those ugly little buggers were swimming around on their own. Of course I can't take all the credit. The packaging is pretty mesmerizing, with its buxom lady Sea Monkeys and buff, King Neptune-like guy Sea Monkeys.

"Will they get any bigger?" he asked, his nose touching the rim of the jar.

"They might. Depends on if I want them to get bigger."

The Sea Monkeys died within two weeks. Cursed, I told Jimmy.

How I proved to Jimmy that I was a warlock (the last time):

I was spending the night at Jimmy's house. We slept on the floor of his room, in sleeping bags. On his walls were *Star Wars* posters. A vinyl E.T. doll was on his bed propped against the wall.

We zipped our sleeping bags together. A satin and down time-traveling machine. A portal, taking us to the land of witches and warlocks.

I told him that Tabitha was a close, personal friend of mine and that sometimes she visited me in my sleep. That Tabitha was no longer a little girl but now she was around our age or maybe older and really pretty. I said that since I was training him to be a warlock now, he would also be visited by Tabitha. Jimmy slept with a blanky—it smelled sweet, like piss and oatmeal—and it lay, like an uncoiled snake, between our bodies.

Now I'm fifteen and Jimmy's fourteen and we're in the same Spanish class in high school. I haven't seen Jimmy in three years—his family's machine shop business boomed and they bought a nicer, bigger house about ten miles away. Maybe they even got a Clapper. Our teacher, Mr. Franklin, calls his name, but now he's James, not Jimmy.

Mr. Franklin—or Señor Franklin as he wants us to call him—has been teaching this class for eons. His white oxford button-up shirts have crusty yellow stains in the armpits, and he always has a chalk line across his butt from leaning against the chalkboard. I didn't take Spanish my freshman year so now I'm suffering through it with a bunch of idiot kids who are still going through puberty—greasy faces and squeaky voices eager to answer questions. In the second week of class, Señor Franklin calls on me and I say, "*Yo no comprendo.*" I don't understand. The class laughs. Jimmy looks at me with that same squint. A look that says, *I know you*, and then he turns to face the front of the room.

Jimmy comes up to me after class. He's taller now, and tan. His neck is long and he's wearing a puka-shell necklace. He must be a surfer, I think. His hair is spiked on top, but through the thick, shiny gel, I can see he's still very blond. He wears pants that look like pajamas—too big and puffy for him and with lightning bolts in wild colors.

"Hey," he says to me, holding his Spanish book and a Pee Chee folder under his arm. "You used to live across the street from me, right?"

"Yeah. Jimmy, right?"

"That's right. Well, James," he says, tugging on the collar of his T-shirt. He looks around the room, watches the last few students filter out the door. "So, like, you remember you used to tell me you were a witch, and stuff?"

"What," I say. "What are you talking about?"

"A witch. You know. Like on that TV show, with the blonde woman who was a witch. You used to tell me you knew her. And that you were a witch, too."

"You mean a warlock?" I ask. I can see his collarbone and a wisp of white-blond hair peeking out from the neck of his stretched T-shirt.

"Yeah, witch, warlock. Whatever. Remember, you used to do magic?"

"I don't know what you're talking about. Are you sure it was me?"

"Yeah, yeah, it was you. Remember? Sandra the witch on

the TV show?"

"Samantha, you mean," I say to Jimmy.

"Right. Samantha. You remember? She was that hot witch on the show."

"I've seen the show," I say. "But I don't know anything about being a witch."

I turn away from Jimmy. "I gotta go to my class," I say.

I can hear him exhale.

"Warlock," he says behind me to no one, and then he says it again a couple of times under his breath. "Warlock, warlock."

I wonder what he really remembers. Samantha, Endora, Tabitha. The sleepovers. Soft kisses in the middle of the night when his eyes were closed. Tabitha's kisses, I told him. Soft kisses, warm breath. The smell of peppermint toothpaste. His arm across my waist like a seat belt as we slept.

MEDITATION

Timothy J. Lambert

He was trying to think about the tip of his nose, as instructed. It wasn't easy. The nose wasn't a hotbed of sensation or spontaneous activity, like the heart or one's eyelids, for example. He could've touched his nose, or pinched it, but that wasn't allowed. Meditating on his ass, which had gone uncomfortably numb from sitting on it all day, would've been much easier. He tried to wiggle his nose, like Samantha on "Bewitched," which he'd never been able to do, but he tried to do it anyway. Instead of moving side to side, his nose did an up and down bunny thing. The Dharma Servers at the Vipassana meditation center had asked everybody not to move, so his bunny nose felt like an imperceptible rebellion.

Without moving his head, he allowed his eyes to dart around the room. The tiny winces and small squirms of the people around him as they tried to get comfortable on their cushions confirmed their agony. It was surprisingly painful to sit upright on the floor all day. Luckily, countless childhood hours spent as a practicing Catholic, as well as many years as a violin student and his recent interest in yoga, prepared him well for seventeen hours a day of meditation. He had felt spasms of pain in the muscles around his spine after his first full day, but now he managed to live with the pain. It had become an acceptable annoyance, like traffic noise or a visiting relative. *Maybe my enlightened self is a masochist.* This thought almost made him laugh and he guiltily looked around to make sure nobody had noticed.

A man six cushions to the left and one row ahead quickly looked forward and resumed a passive state. Had he been looking? Did he see him giggle? Was he gay? He was attractive. Wasn't he? He tried to get a good look at the man, but he was staring blankly forward again. It was hard to tell. All he could see was a formidable jaw, a well-manicured sideburn, and James Dean hair. He looked like a corn-fed Midwestern guy. His earlobe was detached. Wasn't that a sign of intelligence? Hadn't he read that in a magazine once? Did he renew his subscription to *Men's Health* last month?

Shut up! He had mastered sitting still all day, but stifling his inner voice remained a problem.

A tinny whine whizzed past his left ear. He stifled the urge to swat at the mosquito as it lazily landed on his leg. Having vowed to follow the Vipassana Code of Discipline, he wasn't allowed to kill any living beings. He watched as the mosquito bit him; its body ballooned, filling with his blood. Then it stopped drinking, staggered a bit and flew away.

A place like this must be paradise for a mosquito, he decided. *You can eat all you want and nobody tries to kill you. I wonder if all the mosquitoes tell each other about places like this. Maybe Vipassana meditation centers are vacation destinations for the mosquito set. But we can't eat meat, so our blood is probably inferior.*

A bump formed on his leg and he immediately wanted to scratch. *Must not scratch, must not scratch, must not scratch,* became his mantra. He distracted himself by glancing at Corn-Fed Guy. He was wearing a T-shirt with the sleeves cut off. *It's hot in here. If I were allowed to move, I'd rip the sleeves off my shirt, too.* He admired the man's deltoids, his biceps, and wondered about the tattoo on the back of his arm. It looked like a star, but he couldn't be sure. He decided that Corn-Fed Guy was sexy in a dirty way, like a mechanic or longshoreman fantasy character in a pinup calendar. He amended his previous thought. *If I were allowed to move, I'd rip the rest of* his *shirt off.*

However, the Vipassana Code of Discipline also forbade all sexual activity, and he wasn't allowed to move, so anything involving the removal of Corn-Fed Guy's shirt was off the table. Simply thinking about sex probably counted as sexual activity. Which, of course, meant that his mind immediately conjured up nothing but illicit thoughts and images.

He tried to remember what he'd been taught. That all sensations are temporary, that everything will change. Like the itch he couldn't scratch, his thoughts about sex with Corn-Fed Guy would supposedly fade. Unfortunately for him, his leg still itched an hour later. He combated the stinging feeling by gritting his teeth and counting to ten in his head. Upon reaching the number ten, he'd think the word *Balls* as loudly as possible. For some reason, this diverted his attention from the itch.

A loud gong signaled the end of the day. After a half hour of permitted question time, the participants were allowed to resume silence and go to the dormitories. Sounds of footsteps and shuffling feet filled the large common area as people filed outside. A few people grunted and moaned as they yawned and stretched, prompting the Dharma Servers to shush them and gently reprimand them for making noise.

He slowly stood from pillow thirty-four and, while stretching his arms above his head, realized Corn-Fed Guy—who was even more attractive head-on—was looking at him. Even though it was forbidden interaction, he raised his eyebrows, hoping to convey what he was thinking, which was, *What the hell have we gotten ourselves into? Want to sneak out and drive to Vegas and get married?* He was pleasantly surprised when Corn-Fed Guy smiled and pantomimed exhaustion.

While leaving, he faltered at the door, pretending to adjust his shoe, so Corn-Fed Guy could catch up. The fresh air and night sky beckoned from beyond the door and seemed refreshing after spending so much time inside. He wished he could go jogging. Of course, like everything fun, that wasn't allowed. A white sign next to the exit read BE HAPPY in bold red lettering. *How ironic*, he thought.

He casually resumed walking when Corn-Fed Guy caught up with him. Even though they were in a line of others walking to the men's dormitory, he could almost pretend they were the only two on the moonlit path. He wanted to take Corn-Fed Guy's hand, guide him to the garden and get lost in the hedge maze for a few hours. But they parted and went to their respective rooms.

All night he lay on his mat and wondered why he felt so strongly about a stranger. Was it because it was forbidden? Was it the unknown that made Corn-Fed Guy so tempting? What if he had a funny voice? Would that be a turn-off? What would it take to make him unappealing? He thought about his past relationships and realized it wouldn't take much. He always thought of himself as picky or discerning. When his friends asked why he was single, he'd answer that he hadn't found the right guy yet. Was that true?

The next few days were difficult. Whenever he tried to

concentrate on the tip of his nose during meditation, his mind wandered. He felt weak, selfish, angry and defeated. Whenever he looked for Corn-Fed Guy, he felt guilty. By the fourth day at the center he realized his feelings about his inability to concentrate on meditation were a reflection on his life in general. When he questioned whether or not he was wasting his time at the center, he was really being critical about the way he was living his life, the decisions he'd made up to that point in time and his fear that he'd done it all wrong.

It was quite a revelation. But now what?

As he left the main hall one day, he passed the BE HAPPY sign and wondered what it truly meant. He walked silently through the garden and tried to remember a time he'd felt happy. He thought about presents he'd received as a child, but those were fleeting moments of happiness as a result of material gifts. He remembered riding a roller coaster and feeling free with the wind in his face, the excitement that mingled with fear of the unknown, the danger, but was that happiness? It certainly seemed like a metaphor for his past relationships. He thought about his friends, his family, his dog and all the moments in his life when he enjoyed their company, their comfort and the safety of knowing they were a part of his life and would be no matter what. But did that make him happy?

He stopped short on the path when he realized, because he was lost in thought and not paying attention, he was about to run into someone. The other person did the same, and he looked up to see Corn-Fed Guy's surprised expression. The accepted response in this situation by most attendees at the center would be to silently step out of the way and proceed onward. He was about to do that but was distracted by Corn-Fed Guy's smile. He didn't need an exchange of words to know that he was happy to see him, and vice versa, but it would've been nice to be able to say, "It's good to see you again." He hoped grinning in return would convey what he felt.

Which was what, exactly? He spent the next few days thinking about it. Instead of going beyond his nose and advancing to meditating on the rest of his body, like everyone else around him, he thought about what he wanted in a partner. He tried to go beyond the exterior and wished for someone intellectual, empathetic and kind. Someone who gave a damn about the world, who was opinionated, but could respect others' points of view, and who could be serious, but also have a sense of humor. He applied what he'd learned so far at the Vipassana center and wondered if there was a man out there who could be happy just to sit in the same room with him and enjoy his company.

Soon he gave up on imagining his perfect mate and concentrated on accepting himself in the moment. Largely, he was content. He liked his job, he felt secure, he almost owned his house, he had friends and he had just quit smoking. He was perfectly average, and that was okay. He concentrated on his breathing and felt as though he were walking down a long, dark corridor; his destination was a dim light coming from beneath a door. It seemed to take hours to reach it and when he finally did, he turned the knob, opened the door and found absolutely nothing.

He didn't think he had yelled when he toppled from his cushion and his head hit the floor, but he couldn't be sure. He wasn't even sure he'd recognize the sound of his own voice anymore. His chest was heaving, he was gasping for air and sweat beaded on his brow. Somehow, he felt cold in the warm communal hall. He righted himself and resumed his perch on pillow thirty-four. He looked sheepishly at the Dharma Server leading the meditation, but there was no reprimand or encouragement to be found.

A gong sounded, and as the session ended and everybody filed out of the hall, the Dharma Server motioned for him to come forward. *Here we go*, he thought. *He's going to kick me out for disturbing the peace, for bothering the real meditation students and for being a fraud.* Instead, the Dharma Server simply asked, "What's wrong? Is something holding you back?"

He tried to answer, but couldn't form any sound. It wasn't from lack of practice, he knew, but because he was aware that words didn't matter. He felt relief. He wept.

"This is wonderful. You've achieved so much. I think you've gotten more out of this course than anybody else. Tomorrow is your last day. Make the most of it. Be happy."

He saw Corn-Fed Guy the next morning in the dormitory, toothbrush and toothpaste in hand, obviously going to the bathroom. He didn't make eye contract, pretend he hadn't brushed his teeth earlier or contrive a way to be near him as he might have done in the past. Instead, he accepted that what would be would be. *Que sera, sera*, he thought. *Doris Day is my guru.*

During their final meditation session, he thought about eating steak and eggs, walking his dog, reading a book, jogging in the park, reading email, meeting friends for lunch, going to a museum, dressing up and going out to dinner, attending the symphony, and resting his body in his luxurious bed at home. Then he thought about doing those things again, only with a boyfriend.

Yes, that would be better. He felt open.

When it was all over, the vow of silence was still in effect. He walked with the others down the paths, past the gardens and beyond the entrance pagoda. He had assumed he'd run from the center. Instead, he felt like he was walking toward something. Either way, he realized he was walking next to somebody, and that somebody was Corn-Fed Guy. They walked in silence until they reached the parking lot, where they set down their bags and turned to each other.

"That sucked. Want to get some coffee?"

SYMPOSIUM

Andrew Holleran

The accommodations we've been given are two miles from the beach—though gay guesthouses in Fort Lauderdale are mostly near the ocean: those motels from the fifties with high walls or stands of bamboo that make it impossible to see what's going on inside.

What is going on inside this one is nothing; it's Sunday night and it has just rained, so there is no one about. A young man from the reception desk is escorting Maroney and me to our rooms through a landscape only homosexuals could create. It is the sort of place that makes you want to apologize for not being beautiful: a designer jungle choking with bromeliads, hibiscus, heliconia, gardenia, crotons, banana trees, and palms so rare they look prehistoric. This is incredible, Maroney whispers to me as we walk past hot tubs, gym, Internet lounge, swimming pool, lap pool, bike rack, and guest rooms. I don't feel up to this.

Neither do I. We have just come from a panel, reception, and book signing, and are too tired to even react when we finally arrive at a gray two-story building at the rear of the compound, where the young man opens a door and invites Maroney inside.

We'll talk, Maroney says, and disappears. Five minutes later the man from the reception desk emerges and walks me to the opposite end of the building where he opens the door to a circular foyer from which a set of spiral stairs ascends to a high-ceilinged living room so enormous that I ask if this is the common area for a group of rooms that I will share with others, only to be assured that it is all mine.

Fatal words! There is no loneliness like that of a luxury suite! On the main floor are a big kitchen, dining room, living room, and bathroom; up the stairs, a bedroom with walk-in closets and bathroom, and outside, a terrace overlooking the lighted towers of downtown. There is a bottle of champagne in ice on the kitchen counter, in the bedroom a stack of DVD porn in a wicker basket with condoms and folded hand towels, beside the bed a stack of *Architectural Digests,* on another table, books of photographs of Rome, Paris and Rio de Janeiro. The furniture is a cross between Spanish Inquisition and Pier One. The thermostat is set so low it brings to mind a line of Diana Vreeland's: "Air-conditioning is like love—in the wrong hands, it can kill you."

We are here because there are enough retired men in Fort Lauderdale to have founded a gay archives and library that flies people down to appear on panels to discuss the past, present and future of gay books. The audience for the panel was mostly men of a certain age: mine. Giving my speech, I looked out on a sea of white hair on which, like atolls, young men floated, one a geek with black hair and glasses, the other a tall, gangly fellow in a red baseball cap, with broad shoulders, long arms, and enormous hands, sitting with a man who, I was told, produces porn videos—like the DVDs in the tasteful wicker basket before me, a basket carved, no doubt, in some indigenous village in Panama—the sort of thing I can see Maroney writing an essay about already.

Maroney ended his address with a peroration on the importance of the gay literary tradition, even in the digital age; and then, moved by the crowd, connected that somehow to the importance of Love, as he inevitably does. We must believe in Love on some level, he said; the prospect of Love provides Hope; and Hope is essential to Life—every time we go out, to a bar or bathhouse or dinner or club, we are only looking for one thing: attachment to another human being. The DNA of these talks is encoded, he says, he is no longer in control at that point, he can only follow Love's script. At the end they brought us cakes to celebrate the thirtieth anniversary of our first books, which was touching, though half an hour later—it's always the way—I am standing in a hotel room looking through the porn.

The reason, Maroney says, is that whatever form of love exists between an author and his audience is a love that cannot be given physical expression. That's why you meet readers, shake hands, ask them about themselves and then find yourself alone in a hotel room. One minute you're signing books, the next they're gone, as if whatever your work means to these people is in the end only an illusion. There are of course authors—I won't name names—who sleep with any attractive man who makes a point to sit in the front row at their readings. I did it once in Cleveland, and it was a disaster—like telling a five-year-old there is no Santa Claus! Maroney has never done this. The relationship between author and reader, he says, is like that between doctor and patient, priest and parishioner, psychiatrist and client—a boundary one must not cross. That is why, he says, after the applause, the cameras, the questions and answers, you end up in a hotel room wondering: Is it too late to order cheesecake?

A cheesecake would be fattening, so I begin sifting through the non-caloric DVDs, some of which were new when I was in my twenties. Of course, old porn is best, it has a certain innocence. But just as I am about to start the movie the phone rings. It's Maroney saying, Can you help me? I can't get the DVD player to work.

His suite overlooks the lap pool, flecked with wisps of vapor after the rain. When I insert the DVD he's chosen and turn the television to Channel 3, we get snow.

It's always the way, he says. The DVD player will not let me have sex.

Why don't you call the front desk? I ask.

Because I don't want the person at the desk to say, Dermot Maroney just asked me how to run a porn video.

Oh, don't worry, I say. The young have never even heard of us—few of them read.

I cannot take the chance, says Maroney. The young need to look up to their elders. Gay life is already depressing enough. Besides, at this point it's not a case of my reputation, it's a case of protecting the brand.

Then that's that, I say, as I hand him the remote control.

He places it on the little wicker basket filled with DVDs, condoms, lubricant and hand towels. Doesn't this all remind you of Gatsby's shirts? he says.

The ones Daisy weeps over?

Yes, he says. All of America is in that scene!

Maroney could recite *The Great Gatsby* by heart. In fact, his first book was accused of being a mere gay version of same;

both are about romantic melancholy, a longing that cannot be fulfilled.

And now, he says, will you shave my back?

Certainly, I say.

He assumes a position in the middle of the newspaper on the carpet, removes his T-shirt and hunches his shoulders, like a man about to be beaten, or a sheep about to be shorn. I draw the shaver slowly across his back and my thoughts take a sentimental turn to all the years we have been doing this since we formed our writing group in the Village, all the readings, all the panels on which we pondered the question, Is There a Gay Sensibility?

We never found out—and in the end nobody cared; after the boom years, when publishers thought they had discovered a new market, came the bust, when they decided they had not, and not long after that the gay bookstores began closing, one by one, till the only panel we wanted to be on would have addressed the question, What Has the Computer *Not* Destroyed? But we go on, accepting all invitations, reuniting at festivals, where at some point Maroney always calls me from his room to ask not what the future of gay literature is but whether I will come over and shave his back.

Shaving the back is a calming ritual: placing the newspaper on the floor, picking it up when it is over and tossing the shaved hairs into the wastebasket—the wastebasket of our lives! By now I know the contours of Maroney's shoulder blades, which moles to avoid, when to tell him to hunch forward, when to stand up straight; how firmly and at what angle to press the shaver against the flesh, and when I have met his standards. Grooming, among the apes, is a form of bonding.

The job done, Maroney puts his T-shirt back on and picks up one of the books on the table: a collection of photographs of Istanbul.

The trouble is, Maroney says, that by the time you think, I should see Istanbul before I die, the next thought is, Why bother? I can't get laid.

We go out into the dripping jungle to look for the others.

They have made this place into a Deer Park, a garden of earthly delights, a Xanadu. But by the time we leave, we will have learned where everything is, and it will seem small.

That's the progression of Life, Maroney says, a steady process of disillusion.

The wooden walk is wet, raindrops drip from the hibiscus and gardenias. There is nobody out. We find the gym—empty. There is a Coke machine, a bicycle rack with bikes, a cozy library. Mist rises off the turquoise surface of the main swimming pool. There are fresh white towels stacked on tables under a blue-and-white-striped canopy. There is a hot tub on a patio in a clearing. We pass a building where we can see into people's rooms. A man our age lies naked amidst the chintz, watching TV—while, in the adjacent room, a young man stands at a counter, shaving, his muscular back a perfect V shape—which makes you want to tap on his window and tell him to go next door.

These places are torture, Maroney whispers.

Remember the Literature and AIDS seminar in Key West, he says, the one where they took us out on the sailboat for a nude sunset cruise and when we wouldn't take off our clothes the crew didn't know what to do?

Writers, I say. What can you expect?

The last night in Key West, Maroney says, was the worst. I lay awake till dawn while my boyfriend had sex in the hot tub outside our room with other guests.

Why didn't you join him, I say.

I was too much in love.

So what did you do?

I lay there watching the ceiling fan revolve thinking of a fragment of Sappho's.

Which one?

"I lie alone, the Pleiades have set."

He pauses to examine a heliconia.

That's the perfect line for a gay guesthouse, he says as he resumes his tour. And nothing has changed, in all those centuries—except Sappho didn't have a DVD player she could not figure out how to use.

We step over a garden hose.

Key West was the Garden of Gethsemane, he says. What if I had spoken the truth this evening at the library? What if I had told them that the last time I was in love, in mad, passionate, deep and obsessive love, it was so painful that I hope never to repeat it?

He stops to examine a bird-of-paradise. He is beginning to look old. We are the only two left from the writers' group on Mott Street; all the others have died. So we can sit down beneath the canopy by the pool to brood without having to talk. There are stacks of fresh towels everywhere. We sit there with our thoughts, while the rain drips from the orange trees around us. Then Maroney touches my arm, and I look up to see a figure emerge from the jungle on the other side of the pool: a twenty-five-year-old blogger from Miami whose novel about South Beach was written à la Japanese entirely on his smartphone—a young man invited to the conference, we suspect, to lower the average age of the people on the panel—texting as he wanders past the pool with the somber, distracted air of Lady Macbeth. He is dressed entirely in black, his sole fashion statement a studded dog collar—a collar that has made the major question of this gathering whether his master, or someone else, created the big red splotch on his slender and otherwise unblemished neck.

Look, Maroney whispers, he has another hickey.

The young man in the dog collar stops to text beneath a big blue umbrella.

He's very handsome, says Maroney. And the dog collar is so romantic. But that Queer Theory he was pushing on the panel. I think Queer Theory is a form of drag. Discursive practice—sites of contestation—heteronormative!

The young man from Miami puts the phone to his ear.

Let's ask him, says Maroney.

About Queer Theory?

About the dog collar.

But at that moment the object of our curiosity vanishes, like a big black butterfly, into the rain forest.

We get up, go back to our building and agree to meet in an hour—enough time to masturbate, Maroney says, but not enough to color one's hair. Instead I take off my clothes and run around the suite, thinking of a bestseller years ago called *The Lonely Lady*. That's me. I lie down and wait for an idea for a novel to come to me. The phone rings. What are you doing? Maroney asks. Waiting for the Holy Ghost, I say. I'm going to the Jacuzzi, he says.

But there won't be anybody there, I point out.

All the better, he says. Because I just saw myself in the mirror. The penis is out of the question. It really does shrink as you age.

I get up and examine myself in the mirror. That's what hotels are for: ruthless objectivity. They are also for pleasure, and I don't know what to do with all this space and luxury. So I put on my bathing suit and run around, sitting in this chair, then the next. There is a knock on the door. It is the publisher from New York. He is drunk. The publisher is thirty-five, pale white, with a shock of prematurely gray hair and glasses with thick black rims. He has flown down from New York for this event and will fly back tomorrow, whereas everyone else, eager for a free vacation, is trying to get the guesthouse to give him an extra night. The publisher has no interest in life outside Manhattan; his idea of happiness involves cigarettes, martinis, taxicabs and bars. I have never seen the publisher in anything but a suit and tie, but he stands before me now in bathing trunks printed with tiny red starfish and turquoise flip-flops, a navy-blue towel over his shoulders, though it seems appropriate when the publisher informs me that he has a penthouse on the opposite side of the jungle.

Where is Maroney? he says.

The hot tub, I say.

We set out together. The publisher was recently let go by a prestigious house when it was swallowed up by a German conglomerate, and has now, after six months on unemployment, decided to start an imprint of his own—an imprint devoted entirely to gay books. He is after Maroney to give him something. Maroney thinks that if he did, it would give this new venture credibility, but it would also mean a step backward for a writer like himself, a plunge into the *cenote* of gay lit, where mid-list writers disappear, like Mayan virgins sacrificed to the gods.

Maroney is lying on his stomach on a chaise longue when we get there, exposing his shining back to the moon, as he listens to a British scholar who has written a history of the homophile movement in pre–First World War Germany; while the young man from Miami who was invited on the panel to water down its geriatric quality sits beside them texting. Next to them is our warm and winning host, the president of the archives, a retired television producer from L.A. who wrote a novel thirty years ago that he has always wanted to get published and is now rewriting for the umpteenth time.

The publisher orders Cosmos for everyone.

During the brief interlude while we wait for the cocktails to arrive the British scholar tells Maroney that his remarks on the significance of Love moved him; Maroney, self-flagellator that he is, says he always feels like a hypocrite after he says such things.

Why? says the scholar.

Because I think it's something we shouldn't even talk about. It's too sacred. I can't even use the word in real life.

You can't say, "I love you"?

No. It's Wittgenstein. Of that of which we cannot speak, we must pass over in silence.

Then tell us about publishing, our host says to the publisher.

I will, says the publisher, if you first tell me about the baths.

Now there's an interesting subject, says Maroney.

I don't go to the Club Baths, says our host. I go to another baths between a pet store and a Carpet Barn, in a strip mall on Sunrise. But when I go there people fling themselves at me, he says in a detached voice that cancels any thoughts that he is boasting. I mean, I'm overweight, my hairline's receding, I wear glasses—

And you're Daddy, says the young man from Miami.

I guess, says our host.

That's what gay men are looking for, says Maroney. That's what Dr. Isay says in *Being Homosexual*. We're all trying to heal the estrangement we felt from our fathers when they realized we were—different.

That seems a bit reductive, says our host.

Maybe, says Maroney. But there does come a time when you really have to ask yourself why you have ended up alone.

Why have you? says our host.

I don't know. But last night I was lying in bed, wondering, *Who do I love?* I mean *whom.*

That's what I want you to write about, says the publisher. Even though gay men seemed to have stopped reading. Even though the mainstream publishers have given up on us, the bookstores have closed and the gay audience has gone elsewhere.

You mean movies and computers, says our host.

Yes. Before gay books, there was no place to read about yourself or your life. Then came "Will & Grace"—and all its spawn.

The publisher puts down his cocktail and says, "Will & Grace" killed gay publishing.

Everything in your country, says the British scholar, seems to end up a sitcom.

You're right, says the publisher. How I hated "Will & Grace." It was so L.A.—so vacuous and bitchy. It had nothing to do with our emotional lives.

But you have to appreciate the challenge they faced, says the young man from Miami. They had to satirize gay stereotypes they knew homophobes would take literally. They had to instigate a discourse within a heteronormative hegemony.

So *not* what you write, says the publisher to Maroney.

If you'll forgive my ignorance, says the British scholar as he leans forward, but then I'm a historian, what is it that you do write?

Wistful longing, Maroney says.

Every writer has a tone, says the publisher. Maroney's is regret.

But, Maroney says, regret is out.

Oh, says the scholar, and why is that?

Gay life is about different things now, he says, it's about marriage, service in the military, adopting kids, "Will & Grace." It's post-gay.

And is wistful longing, says the scholar, pre-gay?

Yes.

But surely homosexuals have as much right to be wistful as anyone else, says the scholar.

Not anymore.

The wistful longing in Maroney's books is about being homosexual, about the impossibility of love between two men, says the publisher.

Which is now considered retrograde, says Maroney.

Then why, the British scholar asks the publisher, do you want to start this company?

I want to start this company, says the publisher, because I like wistful longing and regret! Won't you give me something, he says, turning to Maroney, a book of essays, your collected book reviews? I'd kill to have anything from you on my fall list!

But I don't have anything, mumbles Maroney against the plastic weave of his chaise longue. I'm dried up.

I'd give you cover approval, says the publisher.

Thank you, says Maroney, but I just don't have anything...to say, about love or anything else. *I'm* post-gay.

But your readers *need* something from you, says the publisher, your readers want to know what you're thinking. Gay people need someone to describe this hopeless longing, this demented search for love!

Maroney lifts his head like a plant responding to sunlight.

I just spent half an hour in my room, he says, trying to get the TV to work so I could watch *L A Plays Itself* and I couldn't call the desk to ask for help because I was too embarrassed at the idea that the young people at the desk would know I wanted to watch porn after giving a speech at the community center about love.

So what did you do? says the publisher.

I looked at a book with photographs of Istanbul.

You see, says the publisher. There is still a place for books.

So can I give you my manuscript, says our host.

When I get back to New York, says the publisher. Send it to me in New York. Now I'm going in the hot tub.

The hot tub has been quietly bubbling on the other side of the patio like the entrance to Hell; it glows, like the pool in which nuclear reactors keep the fuel rods at a manageable temperature, radioactive with sex; it gapes, like the reality beneath literature, though all it really contains is a trio of tax attorneys from Atlanta who did not even attend our reading.

The publisher takes off his glasses and puts them on the table.

You won't be able to see anything, says our host.

That's why I'm taking off my glasses, says the publisher. I take off my glasses when I cruise so that everyone is just a blur.

That turns everyone into an Impressionist painting, says Maroney.

Exactly, says the publisher. Not my favorite period, but it has its advantages.

You mean you're like a blind man, says Maroney, groping in the dark. You have to construct the person by touch?

Exactly, he says.

But why don't you want to see the people you have sex with? says the young man.

Because when everyone's a blur, they're better looking.

But do you wear your glasses at the baths? says our host.

I have to wear my glasses at the baths or I'd trip and break my leg, says the publisher. So tell me, he says, those men in the hot tub—are they young or old?

In between, our host replies.

My demographic, says the publisher.

The publisher walks away.

I think it's sad, our host says in a quiet voice, that someone so young and handsome has to get drunk and remove his glasses before he can look for sex, or love, or whatever it is he hopes to find in the Jacuzzi.

It is a beautiful evening; the sky has cleared, the air is soft and balmy. We watch the publisher settle into the glowing tub. The water bubbles beneath the boughs of the jacaranda tree, the sky is full of stars and the twinkling lights of planes bringing more people to South Florida, the British scholar puts his head back to find a constellation and the young man from Miami texts.

I guess I'm not the only one with barriers to intimacy, says Maroney.

What do you mean? says the British scholar.

I mean the people in the hot tub do not seem to be looking at one another—the people in the hot tub are not even talking.

But you don't know what's going on under the water, says our host.

That's true, says Maroney. But that doesn't change what's going on above the water.

What? says the scholar.

The failure of courtship, says Maroney, the separation of sex and sentiment.

Why shouldn't sex and sentiment be separated? says the young man from Miami.

Because what happens is we're left with only sex, Maroney says.

But what's wrong with that? says the young man.

It's isolating, says Maroney. And when the sex drive fades, you're really out of luck.

I just read a book called *The Selfish Gene,* says the young man from Miami. It explains what's going on above and under the water. The DNA inside us wants to survive, and to do this it has to reproduce. And this drive is so powerful that even when it cannot reproduce, when it ends up in a Jacuzzi or in someone's butt, people do incredible things in its service.

Like wear a dog collar, says Maroney.

Like wear a dog collar, says the young man.

Have you never been in love? says our host.

No, says the young man, but I have been in limerence.

What's limerence? says the scholar.

A state of ecstasy that precedes coitus, says the young man— when the person has chosen a mate, and bathes the mate in all sorts of wonderful characteristics. Then, when it's over, you see things as they are. That's really what most people mean by love.

By romantic love, says Maroney. But there are so many other kinds. There's filial, parental, fraternal, spousal, religious, sexual, platonic. He raises his head. Plato said every person is one half of a whole, and is in search of his other half.

Proust, says the young man, said love was an illness caused by jealousy.

Dostoevsky, says Maroney, said Hell is the inability to love.

But if you can't love, says the British scholar, and you can't write...

What is this, says Maroney, *Boys in the Band?*

No, says the young man, it's *Night of the Iguana!*

I'm going to my room, I say.

I'm going to the hot tub, says Maroney.

Why? I say.

Because you shaved my back.

Instead we all fall silent and look up at the stars, while the young man holds his smartphone up to a faint jet trail in the sky and identifies it as Lufthansa Flight 604, arriving in Miami at 11:34—one of his apps.

AFTERWORD

When we called for submissions to *Foolish Hearts,* I had certain expectations. Social debate having shifted over the past few years, I thought the stories might be about weddings, marriage, and children. About bullies, or the continued push for more visibility of gay lives everywhere and the often contentious push back.

While these seventeen stories do include or allude to all those things, what surprised me was how deftly *places* are woven into the stories and hearts of their characters. A Southern front porch. Resort hotels and cozy inns. A pet store. A balcony. A mall. A farm. A summer job. A circus. A spiritual retreat. We see men finding and losing their hearts on beaches and between sheets in Provincetown, Buenos Aires, Mexico City, London, New York, New Jersey, Fort Lauderdale, New Orleans, Vermont, Ottawa. We see them look back to the boys they were in school as they try to understand the places their foolish hearts have taken them.

I've heard it always: *Home is where the heart is.* But sometimes I believe we have it backward. Heart is where the home is. I felt that each of these stories invited me into a heart. Sometimes what I found there made me laugh. Sometimes I cried. I continue to marvel that the heart is a place at once so strong and so fragile.

I hope you are as honored and moved as I have been to have seventeen voices say, "Welcome to my home."

R. D. Cochrane

ABOUT THE AUTHORS

'NATHAN BURGOINE (redroom.com/member/nathan-burgoine) lives in Ottawa with his husband Daniel. His fiction appears in *Night Shadows, The Touch of the Sea, Boys of Summer, Saints + Sinners 2011: New Fiction from the Festival, Men of the Mean Streets, I Do Two* and *Fool For Love: New Gay Fiction.*

TONY CALVERT (deepfriedtony@gmail.com) is an amateur chef, avid fisherman and lover of folktales. When he isn't working nine to five, he's working on his first novel. While he enjoys the single life, Tony believes in fairy tales, happily ever after and Goofy.

CRAIG COTTER was born in 1960 in New York and has lived in California since 1986. His third collection of poetry, *Chopstix Numbers,* is available from Boise State University's Ahsahta Press. Nine of his poems have been nominated for Pushcart

Prizes and his new manuscript, *After Lunch*, was a finalist for the National Poetry Series.

TIMOTHY FORRY is a writer, bookseller and film producer. He coauthored four novels under the pseudonym Timothy James Beck, wrote an erotic vampire novella as Timothy Ridge, and is currently working on his first YA novel. He lives in Connecticut with his partner, Paul.

MARK G. HARRIS (markgharris@livejournal.com) was born during the Summer of Love in Greensboro, North Carolina, the site of the Woolworth's lunch counter sit-ins as well as the birthplace of O. Henry. His work is included in the romantic short-story anthologies *Fool For Love: New Gay Fiction* and *Best Gay Romance 2009*.

TREBOR HEALEY (treborhealey.com) is the author of the Ferro-Grumley and Violet Quill awards–winning *Through It Came Bright Colors*, along with *A Horse Named Sorrow* and *Faun*, a book of poems, *Sweet Son of Pan*, and a short-story collection, *A Perfect Scar & Other Stories*.

GREG HERREN (scottynola.livejournal.com) is the author and editor of over thirty novels and anthologies. His novel *Sleeping Angel* won the Moonbeam Gold Medal for Excellence in Young Adult Mystery/Horror. He writes two mystery series about two different gay private eyes in New Orleans: Chanse MacLeod and Scotty Bradley.

ANDREW HOLLERAN's last book is *Chronicle of a Plague, Revisited*. He teaches writing at American University in Washington, D.C.

PAUL LISICKY is the author of *Lawnboy, Famous Builder, The Burning House* and *Unbuilt Projects*. His work has appeared in *Tin House, Fence, Ploughshares, The Iowa Review, Story Quarterly, Unstuck, The Rumpus* and other magazines and anthologies. He is currently the New Voices Professor at Rutgers University. A memoir, *The Narrow Door,* is forthcoming in 2014.

TAYLOR McGRATH lived in the Dupont Circle area of Washington, D.C., for several years. He is a publicist, an interviewer, an editor, and under various names, the author of about thirty published stories. He lives and writes in Houston.

ERIK ORRANTIA has a Bachelor's Degree in Psychology and a Master's Degree in Counseling. He was voted 2008 Teacher of the Year for his California school district. His first novel, *Normal Miguel,* won the 2011 Lambda Literary Award for Gay Romance.

FELICE PICANO is the author of more than twenty-five books of poetry, fiction, memoirs, nonfiction and plays—including several national and international bestsellers. He's considered a founder of modern gay literature along with the other members of the Violet Quill. Picano also began and operated SeaHorse Press and Gay Presses of New York for fifteen years. Recent work includes *Tales: From a Distant Planet* and *Art & Sex in Greenwich Village.* Picano teaches at Antioch College, Los Angeles.

DAVID PUTERBAUGH received his MFA in creative writing from Queens College, CUNY. A lifelong New Yorker, his stories have been published in numerous anthologies, including *Fool For Love.* Follow him on Twitter @DavidPuterbaugh.

STEVEN REIGNS (stevenreigns.com) is a Los Angeles-based poet and educator. He's a four-time recipient of L.A. County's Department of Cultural Affairs' Artist-in-Residency Grant. He's published two collections of poetry and five chapbooks, and edited *My Life is Poetry: An Anthology of Autobiographical Poetry by Gay, Lesbian, and Bisexual Seniors.*

JEFFREY RICKER's (jeffreyricker.wordpress.com) first novel, *Detours*, was published in 2011. His writing has appeared in the anthologies *Paws and Reflect, Fool for Love: New Gay Fiction, Blood Sacraments, Men of the Mean Streets, Speaking Out*, and others. He is currently pursuing an MFA in creative writing at the University of British Columbia.

ROB WILLIAMS (robwilliams.org) teaches English and creative writing in San Diego, CA. He is the coeditor with Ted Gideonse of *From Boys To Men: Gay Men Write About Growing Up.* His essays and fiction have appeared in the anthologies *Fool For Love, Fresh Men, I Do/I Don't, M2M* and *Not Quite What I Was Thinking.*

ABOUT
THE EDITORS

TIMOTHY J. LAMBERT (timothyjlambert.com) lives in Houston with his dogs Pixie P. Lambert and Penny D. Lambert. As part of the writing team Timothy James Beck, he wrote *It Had to Be You, He's the One, I'm Your Man, Someone Like You,* a Lambda Literary Award finalist, and *When You Don't See Me.* He cowrote *The Deal* and *Three Fortunes in One Cookie* with Becky Cochrane. His short stories were anthologized in Alyson's *Best Gay Love Stories 2005* and *Best Gay Love Stories NYC Edition,* as well as Lawrence Schimel's *The Mammoth Book of New Gay Erotica.* He selected stories for and introduced Cleis Press's *Best Gay Erotica 2007,* edited by Richard Labonté. With R. D. Cochrane, he edited Cleis Press's anthology *Fool For Love: New Gay Fiction* in 2009.

R. D. COCHRANE (beckycochrane.com) grew up in the South, graduated from the University of Alabama and now lives in Texas with her husband and their two dogs. She cowrote five novels under the name Timothy James Beck, wrote two novels with Timothy J. Lambert, and has authored numerous short stories and two contemporary romances, *A Coventry Christmas* and *A Coventry Wedding.* She was coeditor of *Fool For Love: New Gay Fiction,* with Timothy J. Lambert. She currently has two novels in progress.

The Best in Gay Romance

Best Gay Romance 2013
Edited by Richard Labonté

In this series of smart and seductive stories of love between men, Richard Labonté keeps raising the bar for
gay romantic fiction.
ISBN 978-1-57344-902-1 $15.95

The Handsome Prince
Gay Erotic Romance
Edited by Neil Plakcy

In this one and only gay erotic fairy tale
anthology, your prince will come—and
come again!
ISBN 978-1-57344-659-4 $14.95

Afternoon Pleasures
Erotica for Gay Couples
Edited by Shane Allison

Filled with romance, passion, and lots of
lust, *Afternoon Pleasures* is irresistibly erotic
yet celebrates the coming together of souls
as well as bodies.
ISBN 978-1-57344-658-7 $14.95

Fool for Love
New Gay Fiction
Edited by Timothy Lambert and
R. D. Cochrane

For anyone who believes that love has left
the building, here is an exhilarating collection of new gay fiction designed to reignite
your belief in the power of romance.
ISBN 978-1-57344-339-5 $14.95

Boy Crazy
Coming Out Erotica
Edited by Richard Labonté

Editor Richard Labonté's unique
collection of coming-out tales celebrates
first-time lust, first-time falling into bed,
and first discovery of love.
ISBN 978-1-57344-351-7 $14.95

Men on the Make

Wild Boys
Gay Erotic Fiction
Edited by Richard Labonté

Take a walk on the wild side with these fierce tales of rough trade. Defy the rules and succumb to the charms of hustlers, jocks, kinky tricks, smart-asses, con men, straight guys and gutter punks who give as good as they get.
ISBN 978-1-57344-824-6 $15.95

Sexy Sailors
Gay Erotic Stories
Edited by Neil Plakcy

Award-winning editor Neil Plakcy has collected bold stories of naughty, nautical hunks and wild, stormy sex that are sure to blow your imagination.
ISBN 978-1-57344-822-2 $15.95

Hot Daddies
Gay Erotic Fiction
Edited by Richard Labonté

From burly bears and hunky father figures to dominant leathermen, *Hot Daddies* captures the erotic dynamic between younger and older men: intense connections, consensual submission, and the toughest and tenderest of teaching and learning.
ISBN 978-1-57344-712-6 $14.95

Straight Guys
Gay Erotic Fantasies
Edited by Shane Allison

Gaybie Award-winner Shane Allison shares true and we-wish-they-were-true stories in his bold collection. From a husband on the down low to a muscle-bound footballer, from a special operations airman to a redneck daddy, these men will sweep you off your feet.
ISBN 978-1-57344-816-1 $15.95

Cruising
Gay Erotic Stories
Edited by Shane Allison

Homemade glory holes in a stall wall, steamy shower trysts, truck stop rendezvous...According to Shane Allison, "There's nothing that gets the adrenaline flowing and the muscle throbbing like public sex."
ISBN 978-1-57344-795-7 $14.95

Get Under the Covers
With These Hunks

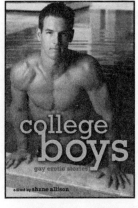

Rousing, Arousing
Adventures with Hot Hunks

The Riddle of the Sands
By Geoffrey Knight

Will Professor Fathom's team of gay adventure-hunters un-
cover the legendary Riddle of the Sands in time to save one
of their own? Is the Riddle a myth, a mirage, or the greatest
engineering feat in the history of ancient Egypt?
"A thrill-a-page romp, a rousing, arousing
adventure for queer boys-at-heart men."
—Richard Labonté, Book Marks
ISBN 978-1-57344-366-1 $14.95

Divas Las Vegas
By Rob Rosen

Filled with action and suspense, hunky
blackjack dealers, divine drag queens,
strange sex, and sex in strange places, plus
a Federal agent or two, *Divas Las Vegas* puts
the sin in Sin City.
ISBN 978-1-57344-369-2 $14.95

The Back Passage
By James Lear

Blackmail, police corruption, a dizzying
network of spy holes and secret passages,
and a nonstop queer orgy backstairs and
everyplace else mark this hilariously hard-
core mystery by a major new talent.
ISBN 978-1-57344-423-5 $13.95

The Secret Tunnel
By James Lear

"Lear's prose is vibrant and colourful...This
isn't porn accompanied by a wah-wah gui-
tar, this is porn to the strains of Beethoven's
Ode to Joy, each vividly realised ejaculation
accompanied by a fanfare and the crashing
of cymbals."—*Time Out London*
ISBN 978-1-57344-329-6 $15.95

A Sticky End
A Mitch Mitchell Mystery
By James Lear

To absolve his best friend and sometimes
lover from murder charges, Mitch races
around London finding clues while bed-
ding the many men eager to lend a hand—
or more.
ISBN 978-1-57344-395-1 $14.95